# OTHER TITLES

## THE DEADWOOD HUNTER SERIES
Lexia

Whispers of Darkness

Holocaust

## THE NEW DAWN NOVELS
Winter Wolf

Wolf Dancer

A NEW DAWN NOVEL

RACHEL M. RAITHBY

SKYSCAPE

**SKYSCAPE**

Published by Skyscape, New York

www.apub.com

Amazon, the Amazon logo, and Skyscape are trademarks of Amazon.com, Inc., or its affiliates.

ISBN-13: 9781503949768
ISBN-10: 1503949761

Book design by Regina Wamba of www.MaeIDesign.com

Printed in the United States of America

*This one's for you, Mum.*
*No. 1 fan and PA Extraordinaire.*
*Thank you for everything.*

# CHAPTER 1

Katalina Winter's favorite night of the week was Sunday.

"Turn up the heat, Dad."

"Sure, Kat." He fumbled for the knob with his hand, never taking his eyes off the road.

Katalina snuggled deeper into her white wool coat. Winters in Michigan were brutal, but Katalina had always loved this time of year. There was just something about a crisp November morning: frost and snow covering every surface, turning the landscape into a glittering wilderness. She had always thought winters had a peaceful silence to them.

"So how's it feel to be eighteen, darling?" Katalina's mom asked, turning to face her from the front seat.

"I still have no idea what to do when I leave school," she admitted.

It bothered Katalina, no matter how many times she told herself she still had time. Everyone else knew where they were heading, what job they wanted, which college to go to, but Katalina still couldn't picture herself in the future. Couldn't imagine where she'd be, who she'd be.

"Don't fret, Kat. You'll figure it out." Her mom smiled, turning back around.

Her dad met her eyes in the rearview mirror. "It's all downhill from here, Kat, wrinkles and gray hairs!" He laughed.

"Duncan, don't be mean!" They both laughed.

"Ha, ha, guys." Katalina smiled at her silly parents. She knew she was lucky they'd decided to keep her. They'd found her before her first birthday, and she'd always wondered whether she'd been left on Mr. and Mrs. Winter's doorstep as some kind of joke: her eyes, of blue-silver, looked as if they were carved of ice themselves. Katalina had hair that was so light blond it was white in the sunlight, and pale skin to match. She was the embodiment of winter.

She'd been the butt of many jokes, but after a while, she'd come to embrace her unique looks. She loved her parents fiercely and had no desire to know her biological parents. As far as Katalina was concerned, they'd done her a favor, dumping her on her adoptive parents' doorstep. It had been the dead of winter and she'd been left with only a piece of paper pinned to her blanket, a single line on it saying, "Her name is Katalina."

Laughing as her father told more jokes, Katalina looked out the window at the passing trees; she saw a flash of something between them. Leaning forward to rub her gloved hand over the glass, she tried to get a better view.

*Wolves?*

If only she hadn't said a word, she might have gone on to love every Sunday night for the rest of her life . . .

"Dad . . . there . . . there's a wolf," she muttered, pressing her face closer to the cold glass.

"What?" her mother answered. "Impossible. I don't think we'd get them this close to town."

"Honestly, look—it's following the car."

Her mother sucked in a breath as her father signaled to turn into their drive. "Duncan, look. It is a wolf!"

Katalina glanced at her father as he turned his head to look, and that's when it happened. When her life changed forever, irrevocably broken . . .

Wolves, in shades of black to gray, ran out onto the road. There were so many that all Katalina could see was a wall of fur. They didn't move, nor did they attempt to get out of the way. They looked at the vehicle, the glint in their eyes promising death.

"Dad, watch out!" she screamed.

"Shit!" he shouted, slamming his foot on the brake.

The car skidded . . . Her mother screamed . . . Time slowed. As the car flipped, Katalina's body was weightless; for one glorious second, she felt nothing, feared nothing, and then time hit fast-forward.

Her body was tossed like a weightless doll, flipped and smashed, while all around her was noise: smashing glass, groaning metal, terrified screams.

Then there was silence, an endless eerie silence that signaled things were very wrong.

It might have been a minute, or ten, or maybe just a bare second, but in that time, Katalina hung from her seat, her head rushing with blood, her ears ringing, and a constant roll of pain riding through her body. None of it was as frightening as the thought of breaking the silence. Because she knew—she knew as soon as she opened her mouth—it would be over. Her life would never be the same again.

"Mom? Dad?" Her voice was barely a whisper, yet the raspy sound sent a fresh pulse of pain through her head.

"Mom? Dad?" she asked more loudly to the silhouettes hanging from their seats, arms limp and fingers unmoving.

Fumbling for her belt buckle, she unlatched it, falling with a thud onto the car roof. Her heart pounded louder in her ears. Finding hidden strength, she was crawling toward her parents when suddenly she heard a whoosh. The car caught on fire.

Panic seized Katalina. She screamed, scrambling over glass and twisted metal. Barely registering the cuts to her hands and knees, she unlatched her father's belt. He slumped down, a dead weight. "Dad! Dad! Please wake up," she cried, shaking him.

Noises from outside filtered in: the scuff of snow, the low rumble of a growl.

Heat. Heat surrounded her, filled her, and each breath burned. She stretched up to release her mother. Nearly at the buckle, she screamed when the window smashed inward. Squeezing her eyes shut, she gasped as glass cut into her skin.

Pain, sharp and deep, burned through her body. She had only a moment to register the bite of pain before something pulled her ankle and dragged her from the car. Her hands flailed, looking for something, anything, to keep her inside the car, to keep her with her parents.

"Mom! Dad!" she screamed.

Kicking and thrashing, she fought against the unseen attacker. Her foot connected; she kicked again and again until finally, the grip loosened on her ankle. She was nearly free; one more kick and she could crawl away, but she never made the final kick. White-hot pain, instant and all consuming, overwhelmed her. Metal gouged into her side, tearing flesh, devouring muscle. Her vision wavered. She almost blacked out as her body met freezing earth, and then there was nothing but pain.

Blinded by tears, she tried to fight, but her body had grown weak. The sounds of snarling grew closer, muzzles prodded, and teeth nipped. The mass of wolves surrounding her blacked out the sky above. Katalina didn't fight. She didn't scream. She felt strangely detached. *This isn't real.* The sound of heating metal, the crackle and hiss of fire, and the nonexistent cries from her parents couldn't be real; none of it was real.

She was pulled over the snowbank as the car was engulfed in flames, and in the light of the fire the wolves surrounded her, all teeth and bites and snarls. Katalina lay unmoving as they tore her clothes and her skin, her blood seeping into the snow around her. She screamed, but she didn't fight. What was the point? Her parents were gone . . . her life, her home, forever changed.

A distant bark drew her attention. *Arne.*

Katalina's German shepherd bounded over the snow, barking at the pack of wolves. "No, Arne! Go, they'll kill you!" she gasped.

Katalina suddenly found strength. She kicked, punched, and clawed at the snow, desperate to get away.

Arne attacked just as a wolf went for Katalina's throat. They tumbled away, the wolf and Arne, snarling and clawing at each other. With the wolves' attention on Arne, Katalina struggled to climb to her feet, the bite on her ankle slowing her down. She stumbled away, crying for her dog, but she knew she had to run.

For a fleeting moment, Katalina thought she might live through this night. Relief trickled through her but immediately turned to fear as more wolves appeared in the trees. Dashes of gray and silver, streaks of white. A strangled cry left her lips as she sank into the snow, icy terror cutting off the use of her legs. Scrambling backward, her eyes fixed on the scene before her, she watched as wolves attacked wolves, light against dark. They were a mass of tumbling fur and snarling teeth. The burning fire cast a warm glow over the whole scene, making the fighting appear as though a beautiful dance.

Forgotten, Arne limped over to where Katalina sat frozen in shock. Whining, he licked her face.

"Good boy, good boy," she murmured, sinking her hands into his matted fur.

A gray wolf split off from the group and moved toward her. Arne turned, growling, protecting Katalina. She tried to run, only to fall back down. The wolf grew closer, close enough that she could see the intricate pattern of white fur framing his eyes and fanning up to the tips of his ears. A scream built in her throat only to be cut off by a strangled squeak as the wolf turned into a boy.

"Run!" he told her, wrapping his arm around her waist and helping her up.

Too shocked to protest, she leaned against the boy, who was a foot shorter than she was but seemed ten times stronger as he easily supported her. He led her through a stand of trees, Arne by her side. Quiet now, the wolf-boy didn't seem to be a threat.

The cluster of trees led to another street, quiet like hers had been. The boy glanced behind him, muttered something she couldn't quite hear, and then said, "Quick, over here. Find somewhere to hide. I'll come back for you."

He left her leaning against a wall as he ran away, changing into a wolf as he reached the trees. Katalina watched, frozen and wide-eyed, wondering whether she'd lost her mind, but the sounds of fighting wolves growing closer snapped her into action.

With the wall for support, she limped her way down the street and up a drive, her hand clamped over her side where the metal had torn into her flesh. Warm blood slowly seeped through her fingers and soaked her torn coat. She briefly thought of knocking on the door for help, but she wasn't sure she could explain what had happened. *How do I explain the wolf-boy?* Creeping quietly past a house, Katalina made her way into an old shed. She sank to the floor behind a stack of boxes. Arne sat beside her, his warm body thawing her frozen one. Shaking, she listened for the sounds of wolves or anyone coming, but heard only the frantic boom of her heart and the shallow pants of her breathing. Burying her face in Arne's coat, Katalina cried. She couldn't quite believe her parents were dead, that this night was even happening; but the hum of pain and the slow trickle of blood through her fingers were a brutal reminder.

She felt the rumble of Arne's growl before she heard the creak of the shed door. With her arms tightly around Arne, she slowly lifted her head.

The wolf was twice as tall as Arne; Katalina clung to her dog as he made to attack. "No, boy, it'll kill you," she whispered.

The wolf stopped a few feet away. Katalina stilled, her eyes locked with its. It studied her with its dark eyes, its head tilting ever so slightly. Katalina's heart beat a hard, fast tempo. Holding her breath, she dared not move.

The wolf before her was made up of shades of darkness. With jet-black fur that seemed to absorb the shadows themselves, it would have been invisible if not for the few silver flecks in its eyes and the dapple of moonlight across its back. Silently, the wolf stepped forward, not even glancing at the growling German shepherd in Katalina's arms.

Katalina sat helpless as it moved closer, yet as the wolf gazed at her, she didn't feel afraid. It stepped closer, so close she could no longer hold Arne back. The dog latched onto the wolf's side, yet the wolf didn't seem to notice. Fearless, the wolf placed its head within inches of hers. Just one bite and her face would be in shreds, but the wolf didn't bite her; instead, it looked at her for a second longer. Katalina could count each silver fleck in its eyes, feel its warm breath against her face. She yearned to touch it, to see if its coat was as soft as it looked, but then the wolf was gone, knocking Arne aside as if he were a Jack Russell terrier. Finally, Katalina breathed again.

For a second, she was filled with the desire to chase after the wolf. For just a moment, she felt empty without him. She felt as if he'd taken a piece of her with him. She shook off the feeling, dragging in a deep breath to clear her mind. Unconsciousness called to her, darkness beckoning. She didn't fight as it took over. Clinging to her dog, she drifted off, forgetting the world for a short blissful time.

The next thing she knew, someone was shaking her awake, whispering her name.

"Dad?" She felt drowsy and confused, her head thick and her eyes heavy.

"Katalina, wake up. We must go."

"What? Dad?" She opened her eyes to see the wolf-boy's face hovering above her, his hair in his eyes.

"Can you stand? They're still out there. We need to escape," he said urgently, standing upright and glancing nervously toward the door.

Seeing his face brought back all her memories. Rather than crying, she focused hard on the boy's face. Seeing only urgency and no malicious intent, she forced her voice to work. "I-I think s-so."

He helped her up, wrapping his arm around her waist, but the pain of moving was too strong. Blacking out for a second, she went heavy in the boy's arms.

"Shit, you've lost too much blood," he muttered, trying to keep her upright.

Biting back a cry, Katalina attempted to make her body move, only to find it uncooperative. Arne whined at her side, licking her slack fingers.

"I'm okay, boy," she whispered to her dog.

The boy let out a low whistle, and seconds later someone else entered the shed. He looked to be about Katalina's age. His features were so similar to those of the younger boy holding her, she numbly wondered if they were related.

"What's taking so long, Toby?" he growled, walking toward them.

"She can't walk and I can't carry her," Toby answered with a glare.

With the aid of the gray morning light coming in through the open shed door, Katalina could see they were both naked. She gave a startled yelp as the older boy stepped forward and lifted her easily into his arms.

"Shush," he murmured, cradling her against his chest. "You're safe now."

He carried her out to the street. His feet were quick across the pavement, but his arms held her strongly and steadily. Katalina relaxed against him, studying his determined face. His hair was the same color as Toby's, only shorter; his blue eyes darker and more serious. Toby was now a wolf again. He scanned the street as his companion placed her into the back of a pickup truck, an older man at its wheel. The wolf jumped into the back, too.

"Ready?" the driver called.

"Go!" the older boy called as he jumped in beside Katalina.

Katalina's heart gave a startled leap as she realized Arne wasn't in the truck, too. "WAIT!" she yelled. "My dog, where's my dog?"

Struggling to sit, she looked over the side of the truck. "Arne!" she shouted.

"Shut up! You'll wake the whole street!" the driver reprimanded.

The truck stopped as Arne scrambled into the back, limping his way to Katalina's side.

"Good boy," she murmured, slumping back down.

Banging the roof, signaling go, the older boy looked down at her, brushing hair from her face. "Hey, I'm Cage. Cage Sinclair. I've waited a long time to meet you," he smiled.

The truck hit a bump in the road, sending a jolt of pain through her. She moaned as her head swam, falling back into Cage's waiting arms. Lifting an unsteady hand toward her head, she tried to ease the constant throbbing.

"Shit, those bastards really hurt you. I'll kill every last one of them for touching you," he growled.

Questions buzzed through her mind. *Who are you? How do you know my name?* But she couldn't voice them as she was pulled into unconsciousness.

# CHAPTER 2

When Katalina woke, she was aware of three things: she was warm, she could hear Cage talking to unfamiliar people, and they knew her name.

She didn't open her eyes right away. First, she listened.

"Is Katalina going to recover?" The voice was deep, gravelly, holding an agitated edge.

"She'll make a full recovery. Though it could be slow; the wolf hasn't been triggered yet," replied a soft and gentle female voice.

"Will she have healed by the next full moon?" the gravelly voice asked.

*What are they talking about?*

"Probably not fully, but changing shouldn't be too much of an issue," said the female.

"Cage, did you feel anything?" the gravelly-voiced man asked.

"I . . . no, but she was injured and we needed to get away quickly. There wasn't really time to bond. She passed out straight away," Cage replied. He spoke with a soft rumble.

*He said he'd been waiting to meet me. What does he mean?*

"The dog? What shall we do with it?" the man asked.

*Arne?*

"It's not left her side since she arrived," said the female.

"It was willing to attack a pack of wolves. I say leave it be. She seemed attached," Cage replied.

"Very well, Cage," the man said, sounding bored. "Hang around. You need to be here when she wakes. Karen, if you'll excuse me, I need to go and make sure we have enough protection on the place." His words were polite, but his tone was anything but.

Katalina heard footsteps growing distant.

"I can tell you're awake," a voice—soft and not yet rough with age—said close to her.

Startled, she shot up, groaning as a wave of dizziness overtook her. "Whoa, take it easy, Kat. Do you mind if I call you Kat? Katalina is such a mouthful."

Lying back down, Katalina rubbed Arne's head to settle him. He lay at the end of the bed she was in, his eyes watchful of the boy in the room.

"You're the one who rescued me," Katalina mumbled, recognizing the young boy.

"Yep, I'm Toby." His hair was a sandy brown. It fell forward in messy layers, skimming the top of his blue eyes.

"How'd you know my name?" Katalina asked.

"Oh, well . . . maybe I shouldn't be the one to explain," he whispered, and then motioned toward the door, indicating that people were listening.

"Please?" Katalina whispered.

"Um, okay. Well, that man who was speaking, he's your father . . . I mean your biological father."

"What?" Katalina practically screamed.

"Shush," Toby hissed, looking toward the door. "Look, Kat, I'm not even supposed to be in here. I don't know all the facts. I—"

Toby shut up as the door opened, his eyes widening before relaxing when he saw who it was.

"Katalina? Who are you talking to? Oh, Toby, I should have known you'd sneak back in here! Jackson told you to go home." Katalina couldn't see him because of the door, but she recognized his voice as that of the other young man who had rescued her.

"What, and miss out on all the action?" Toby whined.

Katalina dragged herself upright in the bed. Arne moved from the end of the bed to beside her, his eyes trained on the door.

The door closed as Cage stepped into the room. She was positive that he and Toby were brothers. They shared the same messy, choppy hair, though Cage's was shorter. Their eyes were the same shape, but different shades of blue, their features similar. While Toby still held the lankiness of youth, he was as tall as his older brother, who had the bulkier frame of a young man on the cusp of adulthood.

Cage glanced at her dog and laughed. "Possessive, isn't he?"

Katalina put her arm around Arne and looked at Cage. "Tell me what the hell is going on!" she snapped, needing to know some answers to the hundred questions fogging her mind.

"Wow, okay, no small talk then." He smiled again, but when Katalina didn't return it, he rubbed the back of his neck nervously. "Toby, beat it!"

"Aw, come on, bro. I wanna see what Kat thinks of the story."

"Kat?"

"Yeah, me and Kat are friends, hey?" Toby replied with a smug smile.

Katalina glared at Toby but couldn't help the smirk that crept onto her face. He had such a cheeky smile and the young carefree glint of a boy who hadn't seen the horrors of the world yet.

Fist pumping the air, he walked to the door. "Ha! I got a smile! Catch ya later, Kat."

"So?" Katalina said after Toby left.

Cage approached the bed only to be met by a growl. "Right, okay," he mumbled, rubbing his neck again. "I'll sit over here. That okay with you?" he asked the dog. "Okay . . . well, I'm Cage."

"You told me that in the truck. Explain how you turn into . . . into . . ."

"Wolves? Yeah, I can see how that's a bit hard to grasp. I'm a shifter. I can change whenever I like, not just by the moon. Although, when you change for the first time, it's always on the full moon. I was born a shifter and so were my parents. I come from a long line of pure wolves . . . and so do you."

"Wait. What?" Katalina swallowed the bile in her throat. *This is crazy. Shifters are not real.*

"Shit, sorry, I'm not breaking this to you very well, am I? You are a shifter, Katalina."

"No, I'm not! I think I would have noticed if I turned into a wolf."

"You've never lived with the pack, so the change hasn't been triggered yet. Your parents, they're shifters. They gave you away so you'd be safe. There are people who want to hurt you."

"Abandoned me on a doorstep, you mean!" She felt a lifelong scar surface, one she'd thought she'd dealt with a long time ago.

"I . . . well, that's between you and them."

"Where do you fit into this, Cage? Why did that man tell you to hang around?"

"Let me explain the situation first. There are two wolf packs in Michigan. This one, River Run, and the one that attacked you, Dark Shadow. We've been enemies for a long time, since before you were born, but the hate escalated when you were a baby. They've been trying to kill off our purebred lines and have pretty much succeeded. Yours and mine are the only ones left. You see, shifters can be born, or created from a bite; the purer the lines, the stronger the wolf. Shifters who are born are always stronger than those created, but as their genes are mixed with humans', the wolves' offspring become weaker. That's why purebloods are so important, necessary for our survival."

Realization dawned on Katalina. "Wait a minute. You're not saying I've been brought here because you want me to have little wolf babies with you!"

"Um, I, well, it's not the only reason. Your father always intended to bring you back when you turned eighteen."

"My parents were murdered last night! All because you want to breed purebred wolves?" *They died because I'm a shifter.* She blinked back her tears, gripping the sheets on the bed.

"I'm sorry, Kat. Your father is the alpha, our leader. He decides. I . . . we never wanted that to happen. Your adoptive parents were never supposed to get hurt. The other pack found out your location and we didn't know until it was too late."

"Hurt? They're dead! Get out!" Her body shook, tears collecting in her eyes, but she refused to let them fall. She refused to allow Cage to see her cry.

"Kat . . ." he murmured, reaching out for her.

She looked at his waiting embrace, wanting so desperately for him to be her parents. He might have saved her, she may have felt safe in his arms, but it was because of his kind that her parents were dead. *Because of my kind.*

"Don't call me that. You've not earned the right to call me that! GET OUT! GET OUT!"

Arne barked, jumping down from the bed, forcing Cage back toward the door.

"Katalina, please. I haven't much choice in this either," Cage pleaded.

Her anger left as quickly as it came. A tear trickled down her face as she looked at Cage, who looked as distressed as she felt. Sighing, she croaked, "I just want to be alone."

Arne had him backed up against the door. Cage had no choice but to leave, his hand fumbling behind him for the handle. Katalina relaxed a fraction as the door opened with a click. However, someone else barged in. Cage jumped to the side to avoid a collision.

"What the hell is going on?" the man who'd barged in asked, anger evident in every strained tendon in his body.

Cage looked at the open door and back to Katalina. "Meet your father." He gave her an apologetic look before dashing out of the room.

"Cage!" the man shouted, staring after him.

Katalina looked at the man who claimed to be her biological father. He looked nothing like her. His hair was red and his eyes green. She'd always thought she'd feel a connection if she ever met the people who made her, but she felt nothing looking at this man. He was a stranger and at that moment, more than anything, she hated him.

His eyes focused on her. "What are you shouting about?" he snapped.

*Is he for real?*

"I want to be alone. Get out!" she snapped back.

"Do not talk to me that way. I'm your father. You'll do as I say."

Katalina nearly laughed at the audacity of this man. "You are not my father! My parents are dead because of you. You have no right to say anything to me. Now, GET OUT!"

"Your adoptive parents are dead because of Dark Shadow. You would be too if not for me sending help." His gravelly voice grated on her nerves.

"They only came after me because *you* decided it was convenient to have me back. What kind of father gives his daughter away until he decides he'd like her back to breed? You're sick and you'll never be my father. My *dad* raised me. He was there for me when I was hurt or upset. *He* took me to the doctor when I was sick. My dad supported me. You have no idea what it means to be a father. You claim to have given me DNA, but you look nothing like me. I don't want to know you, so leave me alone." She glared at him with hostility, feeling breathless, her heart hammering in her chest. Closing her trembling hands into tight fists, Katalina waited for him to leave.

He stared, looking a little lost, as if no one had ever spoken to him that way. He looked as if he was contemplating shouting again, but then appeared to think twice about it. Turning sharply for the door, he paused before he stepped over the threshold. Looking back with haunted green eyes, he said, "No, you look just like your mother and she died protecting you. I may have given you away, but it was the only way I could think of . . . to save you."

He left and Katalina slumped back, angrily. She cried out in pain. The tears she'd been holding back burst from her eyes. With a trembling hand, she gingerly touched her wounded side, running fingers over the fabric of the dressing.

Arne jumped back on the bed and licked her face. He lay down beside her and she nestled her head against his fur. "At least I still have you, hey, boy," she whispered through her sobs.

As she stroked his fur, Katalina realized he was covered in bite marks. She looked up and scanned the room; on the far side was a tray filled with medical supplies. As carefully as she could, avoiding hurting herself further, she slipped from the bed. Gingerly testing how much weight her injured leg could take, she hobbled over to the tray, Arne following.

"Let's fix you up, my brave boy," she whispered.

After wiping away as much blood and dirt as possible, she covered what wounds she could with the ointment and stood, surveying her handiwork. "Not a bad job, right?"

Pausing, she tilted her head when she heard the rumble of arguing below her. "Let's get out of here, Arne. I've seen and heard enough." She found clothes and boots set out on a chair for her, and after checking that she couldn't hear anyone behind the door, she quietly opened it and slipped out. She made her way slowly toward the stairs, her leg slowing her down. She bit down on her lip to keep from gasping in pain.

She made it down the stairs and to the front door, her dog on her heels, without being seen. Her hand slowly inched the door handle down, pulling it toward her as voices drifted through the door at the end of the hall. The door creaked as it fully opened. Katalina froze, not daring to breathe, but their conversation carried on.

"What did you say to her, Cage?" her father shouted.

"Nothing. I just told her the truth," Cage replied, his voice irritated and sharp.

"Now, Jackson, give her some time to adjust. She's been through a lot." This was the female voice from earlier—Karen.

"This is such a mess! I wanted you to help her adjust, Cage, but all you've done is make her think I want her for nothing other than her bloodline."

"Well, that's all you want her for, isn't it? Hell, that's all you want me for. Did any of you ever think I'd maybe like to choose who I am with?"

"Cage!" another female gasped.

"No, Mother, I've had enough! Katalina has every right to be upset. I understand why she was given away, but she's lost her parents *and* she's just been told she's a shifter, yet you want me to be all, 'Hi, I'm Cage. Will you have babies with me?' It's fucking stupid!"

The door at the end of the hall opened. Cage stormed out, his face red and fists clenched. His angry steps faltered as his eyes met hers. Kat stared, her brain blank, trapped in his gaze. Her heart was beating a thousand times per minute; her mouth opened but no words came out.

Cage's finger came to his lips, signaling for her to be quiet. He nodded and gestured for her to go outside. Pulling the door closed, he followed her out. Taking her hand, he led her into the trees surrounding the house.

"Where were you going?" he asked when they'd ventured farther into the trees.

Katalina snapped out of her daze and went on the defensive. "Why, are you going to tell them?" she countered, crossing her arms.

"No."

"Oh." Her arms dropped limply to her sides. She felt kind of mean for being so snappy with him. From what she'd heard, he was in just as bad a position as she was. "Well, I want to go home."

He studied her for a minute, his eyes focusing on her injured parts before coming to a stop on her face. "Okay then, if you follow this forest edge until you reach the road, it's about a five-mile walk to the nearest bus stop. I've no idea when the next gets in. If you haven't noticed already, we're in the middle of nowhere. It's at least a half-day's drive to your house. I'd drive you myself, but they'd notice if I took a car." He rummaged around in his jeans pocket. "Here, it's all I've got on me, but it should pay for the bus ride home and some food."

"Why are you helping me?"

"One of us should get to choose our life. I'm sorry if I upset you. I've been told my whole life we were meant to be together. I suppose I was just so excited to finally meet this girl everyone had always told me about."

"So you were just happy to do as they told you?"

He considered her question with a frown. "I was brought up differently than you, Katalina, and, well, I wouldn't mind belonging to someone as beautiful as you." Cage brushed his thumb gently over her cheek and quickly dropped it, as if realizing what he'd done. "Be safe, Katalina Winter," he whispered.

Katalina stood and watched him run deeper into the forest. He jumped and changed into a wolf before his feet hit the ground again. Her mind reeled. Part of her wanted to get to know Cage, and another part rebelled against doing as she was ordered. For a second, she stared at the miracle she'd just witnessed, transfixed by the wolf becoming smaller and smaller in the distance, until Arne whined and nudged at her leg.

"Okay, okay, let's get out of here." Katalina took one last look at the wolf, now just the tiniest speck in the distance, before turning and walking away.

# CHAPTER 3

"Shit!" Her leg gave way under her. Katalina sprawled face-first into the snow, the cold shocking the breath from her. She lay in the piercing cold, feeling the snow bite into her fingers, the chill frigid against her skin. "What was I thinking, boy?" she asked her dog as she sat up with a grunt. "I'm never going to make it to the bus stop, and even if I did, they'd never let you on anyway."

It was tempting to lie back down and not move, to allow the snow to numb her body to the point beyond pain. A trickle of wetness rolled down her face. Katalina so desperately wanted to be home, in her family's front room, watching TV. The fire roaring, its crackle and hiss the homiest of sounds. Only Katalina could never have that again. She'd never have the chance to enjoy another Sunday family dinner, or listen to her parents' playful banter. She buried her head in her hands, tears dripping through her fingers and freezing on the snow. Arne whined, trying to comfort her with a lick and nudge.

"I know, boy," she mumbled through her broken sobs, "I know."

There was a rustle up ahead, further into the woods. Katalina lifted her head, squinting into the gloom of the trees. She scanned the area for movement. Arne growled low, the slightest of rumbles vibrating up his chest. Slowly, she climbed to her feet, her eyes never leaving the woods.

Arne barked.

"What is it, boy?" He positioned himself in front of her. "Show yourself!" she called, taking a few steps into the trees.

The wolf stalked from its hiding spot, eyes wary, hackles raised, its dark fur startling against the white snow.

"You," she whispered, recognizing it as the dark wolf she'd felt drawn to in the shed.

Arne barked louder, jumping forward.

"No boy, come here!" she commanded, stopping Arne in his tracks.

The wolf studied her for what seemed like forever. Katalina couldn't stand the silence anymore. "Are you a shifter, too?" she asked.

He didn't answer.

"You've lost it, Kat, talking to a wolf," she muttered to herself.

Before her eyes, the wolf morphed into a naked boy. "Yes, I'm a shifter, but not from your pack." His voice vibrated through the air, low and brassy, pleasing to her senses.

"So you're here to kill me then?" she asked, surprised at her calmness.

"I should be, but for some reason, I seem unable," he answered, his voice void of emotion.

"That's comforting," she sneered.

"I imagine it is," he stated. His face remained stoic.

Katalina burst out laughing. *Is this guy serious?*

"What's so funny?" he asked, genuinely curious.

"You! Are you always so . . . literal?"

"I'm not sure what you mean."

Katalina shook her head. "Never mind. So if you're not here to kill me, then why are you here?"

"You intrigue me, Katalina Winter."

"You know my name," she said, shocked. *Everyone knows my name.*

"Most know your name but not your face."

"Well, that's something I suppose."

Silence fell between them. He stared at her as intently as he had when he was in wolf form. She found herself taking an unsteady step, an invisible force drawing her to him.

He frowned, looking down at her leg. "You are still injured?"

"I'm f—" Her leg crumpled. She braced for the cold snow, but he'd crossed the space between them in a blur of movement, catching her inches before impact.

Stunned, she stared openmouthed as he set her on her feet. This close she noted every detail. His hair was just long enough to tangle her fingers into, and the urge to do so was a potent thing. His bare chest was a solid muscled wall, and her fingers flexed where they rested, trailing through a smattering of dark hairs.

"Why haven't you healed yet?" he asked, oblivious to her wandering thoughts.

"What? Oh, I . . ."

He leaned forward, breathing deeply at the curve of her neck.

"Did you seriously just sniff me?" she asked, shocked at the strangeness of the past twenty-four hours.

"Yes, I was just getting your scent."

"Scent?" she asked, bewildered.

"Yes."

"Shifters are strange," she muttered to herself.

"You're a shifter, too."

"So I've been told," she grumbled, still hardly believing it herself.

"Though you've never changed, have you?" He continued, not giving her a chance to answer. "Your father left you vulnerable. He has been foolish keeping you away so long. He's left you weak. You'll need your wolf to protect yourself."

"Mmm."

"Why are you out here alone? Unprotected? You should rest. You will need to have healed enough before the next full moon, for the change to go smoothly."

His reference to change had her refocusing on his words, and not on the expanse of his chest. Tired of the wolf talk, she snapped, "I'm going home."

He frowned. "Is that not home?" He gestured in the direction of the old farmhouse from which she'd escaped.

"No, those people are strangers to me. I don't trust them. They took me away from my home."

"You are the alpha's daughter. No one will hurt you there."

"That man is not my father. My father is"—she swallowed the lump in her throat—"is dead."

Wiping the tears from her eyes, he murmured, "Don't cry."

*Don't cry? Don't cry?* "Why not?" Katalina stepped back from his hold, not caring about her wobbling feet. "I watched my parents die last night." She stared at the ground, not seeing the snow-covered earth, but the crash. "Wolves attacked, almost killing me, and then I woke up in a strange bed, with strange people telling me I'm a shifter, and that I need to come back because my blood is pure and they want me to keep the line going. I turned eighteen yesterday. The last thing on my mind is children, and I most certainly will not be told whom I'm supposed to marry. And *that* man who claims to be my father . . . Where's the proof? He doesn't even look like me. For all I know, he's just some nut job."

Katalina sucked in a deep breath, lifting her eyes from the ground to meet his. "What better reason is there to cry?" Her cheeks heated as she realized she'd ranted to a complete stranger and told him things she maybe shouldn't have.

He studied her. "Very well. If you'd like to go home, I'll take you, but first you need to go back and heal."

"What? Really?" She hadn't expected that answer. She'd expected him to run for the hills after all she'd said.

"Yes, that's what I said, isn't it?"

"But why?"

"You intrigue me."

"That's not a reason."

"Yes, it is."

"You are very frustrating," she laughed, surprised she still had it in her to. Around him, things seemed a little better. Her reaction to him was confusing, and Katalina added it to her mental list of things that didn't make sense.

"Am I?"

Shaking her head, Katalina wrapped her arms around herself, trying to get warm.

"You are cold," he stated.

"A little."

"Right, time for you to go back." He scooped her into his arms.

"Put me down!"

Arne barked.

"Shush!" he growled at Arne. To her he said, "You'll only do yourself more damage. I'll carry you back."

"You can't just go around picking people up without permission!"

"Do you have a problem with me carrying you?"

"Well, yes," she muttered.

"Why?" he asked.

"You have no clothes on!"

He laughed at her. It rumbled in his chest and did funny things to her heart.

"You'll have to get used to that. Being naked is just part of life when you're a shifter."

"Aren't you cold?"

"A little, when I'm like this, but as a wolf, no. You'll see how strong and resilient we are, after you've changed."

"I'm not sure I want to be a wolf," Katalina whispered, looking away from his face.

"Now that, Katalina, you have no choice in. Even if you lived away from the pack again, you'd still change. It's a part of you, your blood. You'll feel different after."

"If you say so."

"I'll leave you here. The young boy is coming."

"Oh, okay," she hesitated, not wanting him to leave.

He put her down and ran off.

"Wait!" she called to his distant figure.

He paused, his voice whispering through the trees. "Yes?"

*Shit, what do I say?* "What's your name?"

"Bass. Bass Evernight."

"Bass Evernight," she whispered, liking the sound of his name.

"See you soon, Katalina Winter." His promise wrapped around her, like silk against skin. She held it close to her heart, wondering when they'd next meet.

# CHAPTER 4

"Kat? Kat, are you out here?"

"Over here, Toby," Katalina shouted, dragging her eyes from the spot Bass had just vacated.

"Kat, are you okay?" he asked, running toward her. "What are you doing out here? Your dad is going crazy!"

"He's not my dad, Toby."

He frowned at her. "Okay, let's get you back inside. Can you walk?"

"Yes, if you help me."

As they neared the house, Cage appeared with a look of worry on his face.

"Thank God," he muttered, lifting Katalina off her feet.

"Damn it! Put me down! What is it with wolves and their lack of respect for personal space?"

"You're injured, Kat, and I've only made—Wait, what do you mean *wolves*? Who else are you referring to?"

*Oops.*

Cage leaned forward as if to smell Katalina.

*Oh no you don't!*

Leaning away, she snapped angrily, "Give me some space, Cage, and stop changing the subject. It's not your fault I want to leave."

"But if I didn't give you that money—"

"Whoa, hold on a minute. You helped her?" Toby exclaimed.

"Shut it, dweeb. Not a word to anyone, got it?"

"Yeah, yeah, whatever. I can't believe you helped her and then acted as if you knew nothing in front of Jackson."

"Well, I wasn't going to just tell him I'd given her bus fare, was I? Jackson would have ripped me a new one."

"Hello, can you please put me down?" Katalina said, annoyed.

"Yes, as soon as you are off the snow. I should have never let you go. I forgot you're practically as weak as a human."

"Hey, rude much!"

"Sorry, but until you've changed, you won't have the strength of your wolf."

"Katalina!" Jackson shouted, his face nearly as red as his hair.

"Great," Katalina muttered. "I've changed my mind. Get me into the bedroom as fast as possible."

Cage smiled at her. "Your wish is my command!"

"What were you thinking? You could have damaged yourself further, or worse, been killed! Never leave this house again without permission!"

Katalina put her head against Cage's shoulder, muttering, "Asshole."

Cage choked back a laugh. "She's fine, Jackson, just needs to get back in bed. Watch out," he said, barging past him.

Jackson followed them up the stairs, muttering and swearing as he went. Toby followed behind, quietly laughing.

Opening the door and holding her steady at the same time, Cage rushed into the room and deposited Katalina on the bed. She immediately rolled over, looking away from her outraged father.

"I think we best let her rest. She needs to change out of those wet clothes and get warm."

"Yes, but . . ."

Cage herded him to the door. "She won't go anywhere again, will you, Kat?"

"No," she whined.

A wet Arne pushed past into the room.

"Ugh, that dog needs to be downstairs," Jackson huffed.

"He goes, I go," Katalina snapped, glaring over her shoulder.

Arne curled up on the floor near the foot of the bed.

"He's no harm," Cage added.

"Right, yes. Well, I want you guarding this door, Cage!"

Katalina glanced over her shoulder and mouthed *thank you* to Cage as he ushered Jackson out the door.

*No probs,* he mouthed back, giving her a salute.

With the door closed, Katalina climbed back off the bed and gently pulled off her wet clothes, replacing them with dry ones.

*Maybe some sleep would be nice.*

*****

*Grinding metal, smashing glass, and her mother's screams. "Kat, help us! Help us!"*

*Hair and skin burning, Katalina's surrounded by the sound of howling wolves. She tries to shout, but inhales ash and dust. Her lungs burn. She's nothing but fear, pain, and fire . . .*

*"Kat, help us!"*

"MOM! DAD! DAD!" Katalina woke shouting their names. Her skin felt as if it were on fire. Surrounded by darkness, for one horrible second she thought she was back in the car, trapped, burning.

The door burst open with a crash, the room suddenly flooded in light.

"What? What is it? What's wrong?" Jackson scanned her room looking for danger, his face one of concern.

"Nothing. I . . . it was . . ." She took a deep breath to calm her ragged breaths and racing heart.

"Kat, tell me what's wrong. I heard you shouting for me and I—"

Katalina interrupted him. "I wasn't shouting for you."

"Oh, sorry . . . I could have sworn I heard you shout Da—Oh, right." She saw hurt cloud his eyes briefly.

"I had a dream. I'm fine. You can go now."

Jackson looked at her, unsure of what to do. Running a hand through his unkempt hair, he looked at the floor and then back at Katalina. "I'm sorry, you know . . . it was never supposed to be this way," he murmured.

"*Sorry* won't bring my parents back." She regretted her words the second they left her mouth and yet she still couldn't quell the temper inside of her.

His face dropped, the hard line of his mouth softening. For the first time, Katalina could see the man he must have been, the man with a wife and a child. "I—"

"Look, I'm sorry. I just . . . I don't have room for you right now. I get I'm your daughter, but I've just lost my parents. I'm not ready for another dad and I'm not sure I'll ever be. A day ago, I was happy and I had a family. Now, my world's been turned upside down and I'm all alone."

Jackson looked at her one last time and then switched the light off. She heard the door creak, but before it closed, he said softly, "I'll be here whenever you're ready. If you need anything, shout for Cage. He's asleep on the sofa. I think Toby's hidden himself away somewhere, too. He hates to miss out on the action. You're not alone, Katalina, please remember that."

"All right," she answered, not sure what else to say, or how she even felt about his words.

As soon as the door closed, Katalina let the flood of tears she'd been holding back fall down her face.

Feeling emotionally wrung out, Katalina cuddled up to Arne when he jumped onto the bed. Trying to sleep, she struggled; she couldn't relax, and the longer she lay in the silence of the darkened room, the worse she felt. Slipping from the bed, she crept from the room and across the dimly lit landing to the bathroom. The house was quiet and dark. Fumbling for the light switch, Katalina flooded the bathroom in light and walked to the sink. She turned on the tap and splashed water onto her face.

A headache throbbed behind her eyes and she felt weak and dizzy. Reaching for something to steady herself, Katalina missed the basin and slid to the floor, her head spinning.

"Toby?" she whispered loudly. "Toby?"

"How'd ya know I was here?" he asked, popping his head around the door, a big grin on his face. "Hey, you all right?" he asked, coming into the bathroom.

Her head gave a violent throb. "Ugh . . . ouch! Yeah, I just have a headache. Don't suppose you'd help me up and find me some painkillers?"

"I can get Cage if you'd like?"

"No, no, just help me up. I'll be fine."

"Okay, but I'm not sure, Kat. You look kind of ill."

"Hey," Cage said, his head appearing above Toby's.

"Ugh, what is it with you Sinclair boys, lurking around doorways?"

"I wasn't lurking. I was downstairs. Wolf hearing, remember? Every wolf in this house heard you calling Toby."

"Well, not every wolf in this house needs to be in this bathroom with me, just one."

Her head hurt so much; every sound rattled her brain. *God, I need my bed.*

"Ooh, touchy!" Cage laughed. "Toby, help her up. I'll find some painkillers."

"Thanks." Katalina smiled guiltily. *Maybe I shouldn't snap at every person I meet.*

Toby held out his hand and pulled Katalina up. Walking her back to the room, he said, "I'm beginning to think you only like me for my amazing walking-stick skills."

She laughed at him only to trigger another throb of her head. "Ugh, stop making me laugh." With a hand to her forehead, she climbed onto the bed, curling into a ball to try to settle the throbbing.

"Are you sure you're all right? You feel really hot," Toby said, touching her face.

"Probably just a fever from getting cold. I just need those pills and sleep."

"Ask and you shall receive." Cage smiled as he entered the room and held out a glass of water. Katalina reached for it but the glass slipped through her fingers as her arm trembled. "Steady," Cage murmured, catching the glass just before it smashed.

Katalina looked at him, wide-eyed. "Impressive reflexes."

"All part of being a wolf. You'll see." He smiled. "Do you need a hand?" He gestured to the water and pills.

She nodded, returning his smile. She realized she'd been taking out her frustration and pain on Cage. It wasn't fair of her to do that. He'd tried his best to help her so far, yet there was still a small part of her that was wary of letting him close. Jackson wanted them together, and Katalina didn't have any desire to do as he wished.

Cage gave her the pills, and then held the glass to her lips, his hand behind her back to hold her up.

"Kat, I think we should get Karen to look at you," he whispered, laying her back.

"No, please, I don't want to wake up the whole house."

"I can assure you no one is asleep."

"No, we're not," a woman said, walking in, Jackson behind her.

"How can you ever have any privacy living with wolves?"

"You'll get used to it. I'm Karen, the doctor." She had a warm, motherly smile and a soothing presence.

She held her hand to Katalina's head and then listened to her heart rate. "Hmm, mild fever. Best to take some antibiotics in case you've got an infection. No need to panic, though I think it will be best if you're not alone, just in case."

"I'll stay!" Toby said, jumping up and down.

"Cage will. She needs rest, Toby. You'll be up gossiping all night."

"Ugh! Fine." He crossed his arms with a huff.

Katalina took the antibiotics Karen gave her and rolled over, blocking the others out as they talked quietly near the door. She'd had enough of everyone crowding her. She wished her mom could have been the one sitting by her bedside.

"Cage, keep an eye on her breathing. Call me if it quickens," Karen murmured before shutting the door.

After a few moments of silence, Katalina rolled over to face Cage. She pulled the covers up to her chin as she shivered.

Cage met her eyes. "Cold?"

"Freezing cold and boiling, all at the same time. I hate being ill."

"The fever should break soon. You'll be better in no time. Get some sleep."

"Hmm." Katalina closed her eyes, but all she saw were red flames flicking over melting metal. "Cage?"

"Yeah?"

"Talk to me."

"What about?"

"Anything, just distract me."

"You should really try and sleep."

"I can't. I . . ."—she took a deep breath—"every time I close my eyes, I see them. I see them burning in the car."

Cage didn't comment but took her hand. She welcomed the warmth his hand offered, finding comfort in his touch.

"What do you want to know?"

"Anything—tell me about yourself. How old are you? Where'd you go to school? All I know is you're a shifter and we're supposed to make wolf babies."

"You laugh at that, yet I've been told that for as long as I can remember. Our childhoods were obviously very different. Well, where to start? I'm eighteen, like you, and my birthday is June third. I was homeschooled like most of the pack kids. I'm one of the best fighters in the pack—"

"Why are most kids homeschooled?"

"It's just easier to keep our secret that way. When kids shift when they're young, sometimes they find the change hard to control."

"Isn't it isolating being cut off from the real world?"

Cage laughed softly. "We're not cut off, Kat, but we aren't human. We're shifters. The pack is our family; we look after each other. You've been brought up differently, but that doesn't mean the way I was is wrong."

"I didn't mean it was. I just . . . I'm trying to imagine myself here, and I don't fit."

"Where do you fit, Kat?"

*Where do I fit?* She didn't know. She'd loved her life and her family, but she'd always felt as if she didn't belong. She still hadn't decided what to do when she left school. She'd always put it down to being adopted and not knowing where she came from.

"I don't know," Katalina whispered.

"Hey Kat, I didn't mean to upset you."

Katalina sighed. "I'm fine. It's just . . . I feel like I'm adrift; nothing seems real. I keep waiting to wake up. My parents died, Cage. Two days ago, I was sitting in the back of the car laughing with them, and now they're gone and no one seems to acknowledge that. I feel as if Jackson just expects me to move on and be grateful I have the pack, but I can't do that. I want to go home. I want to say good-bye to my parents with the rest of my family. I don't belong here. I belong with the people who'll understand exactly how I feel."

He rubbed his fingers across her face. "Get better, Katalina, and then I'll talk to Jackson, okay?"

She wasn't sure Jackson would listen, but it made her happy that Cage was willing to talk to him. Yet she wished he'd just take her back home. The thought made her mind wander to Bass; he'd said he'd take her home. *Why is Bass willing to break the rules and Cage isn't? Ugh, I need to stop thinking.*

"Tell me a story, Cage."

"What?"

"Please, distract me. Tell me anything. Something nice, so I can fall asleep."

"Okay, here goes . . . Once upon a time, there was a little boy who was told he'd been chosen for a very special task: when he grew up, he was to marry a special girl with silver-blond hair and eyes of crystal. The little boy grew up waiting for the day he'd meet her, hoping he'd be worthy of her, and when that day finally came, she was more beautiful than he could have ever imagined. They spent the rest of their lives running through the forest as wolves, darting through the trees, happy, free . . ."

\*\*\*\*\*

Katalina drifted off, dreaming about a little boy she wished she'd known, but her dreams twisted and changed, and soon she was back in the car, burning metal all around her and the shadows of her parents, who hung limply in the upside-down vehicle. Someone was shouting her name over and over, grabbing her . . .

"Kat, wake up!" Her eyes shot open. She tried to focus on Cage's face, to leave the past behind, but it pulled her back. She felt as if she were burning, as if she were still surrounded by melting metal.

"Kat, you're okay. It's just a dream." His hands brushed hair from her face, stroking her gently.

"I'm burning," she croaked.

"No, Kat, you're here. You're safe."

"No, Cage, I'm burning. I'm so hot, my head . . . it hurts."

"Okay, okay, I'm going to get Karen."

He whistled low, like Toby had done when he'd found her that first night. Karen rushed into the room seconds later. "Cage, what's wrong?"

"She's burning and she says her head hurts."

Kat tried to concentrate on their voices but her head felt too thick; it was as if there was an invisible wall between her and them, blocking out their voices and blurring their faces.

". . . *infected . . . drip . . . water . . .*" Words floated around her but nothing made sense. She drifted in and out of consciousness. There was a sudden contact of cold against her forehead and it eased the throbbing slightly, while Cage's face came in and out of focus above her.

"Sleep, Kat," he said softly, as more cold touched her forehead.

She didn't want to sleep. She didn't want to be looked after anymore, but her body wouldn't listen and she was swept into darkness.

# CHAPTER 5

Katalina slowly peeled open her eyes. The light blinded her, making her eyes swim with tears. Feeling stiff, she wiggled her toes and fingers. She sat up in bed, looking around the room, feeling a little confused. There was no one with her, not even Arne. A chair was pulled close to her bed; a small bowl of water sat on the bedside table; and a cloth hung half in, half out of the bowl as if it had been tossed there in a hurry.

There was a drip attached to her hand; clear liquid half filled the bag hanging on a metal pole.

*Where is everyone?*

"Toby?" she whispered; he always seemed to be lurking nearby. "Toby?"

The door slowly opened. Toby's grinning face appeared seconds later, followed by Arne.

"There you are, boy," she croaked, her voice gravelly.

"Sorry, I took him for a walk, seeing as he's been cooped up for days." *Days? How long have I been out?*

"What day is it?" she asked, not sure she was ready for the answer.

"Sunday. You've been pretty out of it. Cage just left for a pack meeting he couldn't miss. He's been glued to your side. Sad, really," he laughed.

"What are they meeting about?"

"Oh, not sure. I can go spy if you'd like," he said.

Katalina laughed, shaking her head.

"So are you feeling better?" he asked, dropping into the chair beside her bed. Arne stuck his head on his lap, whining to be petted.

"Traitor," Katalina muttered at the dog. "Yeah, I feel a bit better; not hot, just weak and thirsty. Would you mind getting me a drink?"

"Sure, back in a minute." Arne jumped up and trotted after him.

"Great, I've lost my dog now, too," she muttered.

Toby came back minutes later, a glass in his hand. "Sounds like they've nearly finished, so Cage will be here any moment."

"Hmm." Katalina couldn't quite remember what she'd said to him before being ill, but she remembered the feel of his hand in hers. She liked him; he made her smile and he obviously cared for her, but all she wanted was to get better and go home.

"You know, he's been waiting for you all his life," Toby said, his voice unusually serious.

Katalina whipped her head around, not quite believing he'd said the statement. Toby was carefree; she wasn't expecting such a serious comment from him. "Yes, I can see that. I can see he truly cares for me, but where I come from, people don't choose who they love; it just happens—sometimes unexpectedly, sometimes slowly over many years. I don't want to hurt Cage, but I don't know how I feel about him. All I feel right now is a gaping hole in my heart, from the loss of my parents, from the loss of the life I used to live. I just want to go home. Is that so hard to understand?"

"No, it's not." Cage walked into the room, and by the look on his face, she could tell he'd heard every word.

"Cage . . . I—"

"No, it's fine, Kat. I get it. I truly do, but that doesn't mean it doesn't hurt." He looked at her a second longer before turning on his heel and exiting the room.

Toby looked awkwardly toward the door and then at Kat.

"It's all right, Toby, you can go."

He didn't even say good-bye. Toby was up and out the door in a flash, locking Arne inside the bedroom. He scratched at the door.

"Hey! Come here, boy." Arne came over with a whine, jumping up onto the bed beside her.

Katalina wasn't sure how long she lay staring at the ceiling. Absentmindedly, she ran her fingers through Arne's fur, and when the bedroom door opened again, it wasn't Toby or Cage; it was Karen.

"Hey, I heard you were awake. How do you feel?" she asked with a warm smile.

"Better."

"Fever's broken," Karen said, holding a hand to Katalina's forehead. "I just need to change the dressing on your leg. It was infected—that's why you had such a bad fever. But you're on the mend."

Katalina nodded and stared at the wall, while Karen busied herself with changing the dressing. A heavy feeling sat in her chest, gnawing at her, churning her insides.

"Where have your guards gone? Those Sinclair boys haven't left your side . . . Well, Toby mostly lurked outside because Cage wouldn't let him in." Karen smiled warmly.

"Cage is angry at me, and Toby went to see if he was all right."

"Oh." She didn't say any more, but just carried on applying the cream she held in her hand.

"I don't want to hurt Cage; he's lovely and has been nothing but nice to me, but Jackson has given Cage something that was never his to give in the first place. Only I can give my heart to Cage."

"And you don't want to give Cage your heart?"

Katalina looked at Karen and replied in a sad voice, "I just want to go home and say good-bye to my parents. Why does no one understand that?"

"I understand, Kat. You have every right to feel that way."

"Really? I expected you to be just like the rest."

"Ah, Kat, do not take Jackson's views as the whole pack's views. Yes, we'd like to have our bloodline continue. I personally would love to have you back, but we cannot always have what we want. In a perfect world, I would have never lost my daughter, and you would have been brought up by your mother."

*Daughter?*

Katalina looked at Karen, really looked. "Your eyes . . ."

"Yes, your mother was my daughter. These eyes have been passed down from generation to generation, but only in the females. Your hair, though, you get that from your grandfather's side. Unfortunately, he isn't here to see."

"I don't understand. Why didn't you say who you were?"

"Because, Kat, unlike Jackson, I do not presume that blood makes us family. Family is much more than blood. I'm guessing you already have a grandmother. I have no right to claim that status when I knew you for only the first six months of your life—and what a wonderful six months they were. I'd love nothing more than to have the chance to get to know you, if you'd like."

"I . . . yes, sure, sorry. I just feel a little overwhelmed. The past few days have been so . . . overwhelming."

Karen pulled the covers back over Katalina's legs and turned to pick something up. "I can only imagine how you feel. I'll give you some space. Here, I'd like you to have this. It's a photo album of Jackson, your mother, and you. I know Jackson has gone about things in completely the wrong way, but he used to be a reasonable man, a happy man. When his world ended, he traveled on the wrong path. It's been nearly eighteen years now and no one has been able to steer him right, but I think soon things are going to change."

Karen walked to the door. Sitting in the bed, Katalina gripped the worn album in her hands, her emotions in turmoil.

"What makes you think I can change him?"

Karen smiled fondly. "Because, Kat, you have a fire in your eyes, a fire your mother possessed too, and she . . . she was the only person who steered Jackson in the right direction."

"What was her name, my mother?" Katalina asked, staring at the album.

"Winter."

Looking up, Katalina wasn't sure she'd heard her right. "Winter?"

Karen smiled sadly. "Yes. Jackson didn't just leave you on any doorstep. He wanted you to carry her name."

Karen left the room, leaving Katalina alone with her thoughts.

She ran her fingers over the worn album, the leather faded and wrinkled. She couldn't bring herself to open it. She wasn't ready to see the life she could have had. She wasn't ready to see the mother who never had the chance to raise her.

Feeling suddenly overcome with fatigue, she lay back down, wishing the churning knot in her stomach would go away. Karen said she didn't expect anything from her, but that wasn't true. She not only wanted her to carry on the pure bloodline, she wanted her to save Jackson. Katalina didn't want to know him. She hated him for all he'd done, and she didn't think anyone could make him see he was wrong.

*Only a few days ago, I was happy . . . Oh, Mom, Dad, I miss you . . .*

# CHAPTER 6

The morning sun peeked behind the drawn curtains, flooding the room in a muted orange.

"Knock, knock," Toby said as he opened the door.

"Hey, Toby."

"Brought you some breakfast if you're feeling up to eating."

"Yes, please, I'm starving. Do you think I could get this drip out my hand? Kinda hate needles."

"Karen's coming over at lunch. You'll have to ask her then. She instructed me to change the bag, though."

"You?"

"Oh, okay, she asked Cage, but Jackson had a fit because she didn't ask him. He stomped off somewhere, and then Cage . . . he asked me to do it. I saw Karen change it last week; can't be that hard." He grinned at her.

"Hmm, I don't feel worried one little bit." She started to stuff the food he'd given her into her mouth. "So Cage hates me then?"

"Hates? No, don't be silly. He loves you."

Katalina's eyes widened.

"Well, maybe *loves* is a little strong. He . . . well, he really likes you, Kat, and you kinda hurt his feelings."

"So he stomped off, too?"

"Yep, it's just me, you, and Arne."

"So does this house have a TV or is that too high-tech for shifters?"

"'Course we have a TV. Who doesn't have a TV?" he laughed.

"So can we go watch it? I'm going to go insane if I have to stay locked in this room another day."

Toby frowned, guilt clouding his eyes. "Kat, I can't, but—"

"Oh, come on, Toby, *please*? Don't be a bore. You're the only fun one around here. Pretty please?" She smiled her sweetest smile.

"Ugh, Kat, you are going to get me in trouble. All right, come on then; I'll help you down the stairs."

Katalina slipped out of bed, using the metal stand her drip was attached to as support. "Yes! Thanks, Toby! You're the best," she said, ruffling his hair.

"Hey!" he moaned, ducking. "Don't push your luck!"

"I'll be on my best behavior, promise. Just the sofa and TV—what could go wrong?"

Several hours later, Katalina regretted her words as a police car pulled up to the house.

"Shit!" Toby muttered as Arne barked. "Shit, shit, shit!" He ran his hand through his hair.

"Toby, calm down. You're just a kid. They can't do anything to you. I'll just tell them you saved me if they are here for me. But honestly, how would they know I'm here? It's probably about something else."

Toby looked around in panic and then locked eyes with Katalina. "Stay here! Do not come out, even if it is about you, got it?"

"Toby."

"No, Kat, I'm serious. I might be just a kid but I'm also a shifter, and your dad, my alpha, would kill me if I lost you, and I mean that literally! Or worse, he's probably out there watching the house, and when they take you away, he'll come out and start fighting the cops!"

"All right, all right. You'll never know I was here."

There was a knock at the door. Toby glanced at Kat, looking as if he might be sick. Taking a deep breath, he left the room, shutting the door behind him.

Kat moved closer to the door so she could hear them better.

"Looking for a Jackson Song. Is he here?"

"No, sorry, he's out."

"Are you his son?"

"No."

There was a pause. She could imagine the cop bristling, his feet tapping with impatience.

"Look, son, this is important. There's a girl gone missing. Her parents are dead, and there was a report of someone carrying an injured girl a few blocks over from where she lived. These people saw the girl being driven away in the back of a truck. They got a partial plate number and their description with the partial matches up with one of Jackson Song's trucks. Know anything about that, son?"

"No, sorry. No girl here, just me."

Arne started to scratch and whine at the door.

"Arne, come here," Katalina whispered.

"What's that?"

"Oh, um . . . Jackson's dog. I'm dog sitting while he's away."

"Can I get a look at that dog? This girl had a dog, too. Seems it's gone missing with her."

"Sorry, he's not too friendly with strangers."

Katalina tried to drag Arne away from the door but slipped and knocked into a table. The lamp wobbled, but she caught it just before it fell.

"Let me in, son. I won't be long, just need to do a quick search, make sure she's not here."

"Do you have a warrant?" Toby said, sounding much older than his twelve years.

"Well, no, but what harm is there if it's just you and a dog here?"

"Sorry, sir, but if there is no warrant, I can't let you in. It's not my house."

"Right. Well, when will Mr. Song be home?"

"In a week."

"I'll be back, kid."

The door closed and Toby walked into the front room seconds later. "Seriously, Arne," he growled at the dog.

To Katalina's surprise, Arne whined, going down on his belly in submission.

"Hey!" Katalina patted her leg. "Come here, boy. You don't have to submit to him!"

Arne glanced at Toby and then scurried to Katalina.

She glared at Toby. "That wasn't nice, scaring him."

"I wasn't scaring him, Kat. I was telling him off for nearly getting us caught. I can't believe the cops are looking for you."

"Well, he never cowers on the floor when I tell him off, and what did Jackson expect? You can't just kidnap someone and expect there won't be consequences."

"He cowered 'cause I'm a wolf, Kat, or have you forgotten? And we didn't kidnap you. You are Jackson's daughter. You would have died if we hadn't found you," he snapped.

Katalina looked at Toby and, for the first time, she could see it; he wasn't just a kid with a carefree smile. Underneath it all, he was a wolf, a wild creature.

"No, I didn't forget, Toby. I just thought you were different. My mistake; one I won't be making again."

She grabbed hold of the drip and hobbled from the room. "Heel, boy," she said to Arne.

"Kat . . . Kat, at least let me help you."

"No! I don't need any more help, from any of you. As soon as I'm better, I'll be leaving and there is nothing Jackson can do about it. Just because you're a shifter, Toby, doesn't mean different rules apply."

*****

She heard shouting that night. Jackson was banging and swearing as Karen and whomever else was with him tried to calm him down. Katalina stood at the window watching darkness take over the sky when she saw a glimpse of a wolf dashing away from the house. *Toby*, she thought, and then moments later a larger gray wolf followed.

*Cage* . . . She couldn't know for sure, as she'd never seen his wolf, but if that had been Toby, then it would be Cage following him. She wondered if this was what it was like all the time here, or whether Jackson was acting like an ass because of her. She hoped he wasn't always like this. What a horrible life it would be always tiptoeing around him, trying not to upset him.

"Are you all right?"

Katalina jumped. She hadn't heard Karen open the door.

"Sorry, dear, didn't mean to startle you."

"It's all right. I just didn't hear you come in."

"Don't worry. You'll be able to hear everything we can after the full moon."

"Why is it you all presume I want to be a shifter? I'd love nothing more than to reverse time and never meet any of you!"

Karen didn't answer, but Katalina could see she'd hurt her.

"I . . . I'm sorry. That wasn't fair. I'm just . . ."

"It's all right, Kat. I understand and I am truly sorry for your loss. Being a shifter is something we treasure. I hope you will understand after the change." Karen stared off into space for a second, her mind elsewhere. She snapped her head up, plastering a smile on her face.

"Toby tells me you'd like this drip off. I think you're almost better, so let's get it off."

Katalina sat on the edge of the bed in thought as Karen bustled around her, collecting medical supplies.

"I'd like to change that dressing one last time too, if you don't mind?"

"Sure," Katalina answered, swinging her leg gently up onto the bed. "So is Jackson always like that?"

Karen locked eyes with her. "Did you look through the album?"

"No, I just—I'm not ready."

"Look at it, Kat. There you'll see the man Jackson used to be, the man he could be again."

"I don't understand why everyone puts up with him. Why would they want a leader with such rage?"

"Because, Kat, wolves live by a code of honor and loyalty. He's our alpha and we would die for him. We also hope that one day the man we lost will come back to us." With those words, she left quietly and Katalina went back to staring out the window.

She wasn't sure how long she'd stood there, but when she finally decided it was time to look at the family she'd once had, the moon had risen high into the sky, its crescent shape casting a dim light over the snow-covered world.

Picking up the album and a thick blanket from the bed, Katalina went down the stairs and out the front door; there she sat on the porch steps, the blanket wrapped around her and the album in her lap. Taking a deep breath, she opened it. The first picture was of a woman. She looked to be in her early thirties. She was sitting on a bed with a baby in her arms. Katalina looked at the woman's smiling face, at the happy glint in her eyes and the glow of love for the newborn she held.

She didn't need to read the description to know this was her mother; they shared the same eyes and hair; in fact, Katalina thought it was like looking at an image of herself in another fifteen years. There was no mistaking their relationship.

She turned to the next page and almost didn't recognize the man who stood with her and Winter. Jackson still had the same messy fire-red hair, the same imposing stance, but in the picture, his eyes didn't hold the haunted look of grief, his mouth didn't have the hard set of rage. Jackson was truly happy, his hand gently holding Winter's, beaming proudly at the camera.

Katalina flicked through the whole album, looking at picture after picture of her first six months of life; in every one they were happy, and it wasn't just pictures of Jackson, Winter, and her. There was one with Karen and a man with his arm around her. There was a group shot with a couple who looked as if they were Cage and Toby's parents, and the last was one of around thirty happy, smiling people, Jackson and Winter at the center of them.

Katalina closed the album as a tear rolled down her cheek. Her hands trembled as she hugged the album to her chest. With each breath she took, the pain inside of her grew more intense. She stared out, the darkness a welcome companion. The feelings inside of her were as bleak and empty as the desolate landscape around her. The grief and loss she felt grew by the day, the hollow feeling in the pit of her stomach a constant thing. She wondered if she'd ever feel whole again.

"Kat?" Karen walked out onto the porch. "Kat, what are you doing out here? You'll freeze to death!"

Katalina wiped at her tears. "I won't be long. I . . . I just needed some air."

Karen's hand rested on Katalina's shoulder. "What's on your mind, Kat?"

"Why did this happen? Why do the packs hate each other so much?"

Sighing, Karen took a seat beside her. "I'm afraid this story isn't a nice one. I would love to say we are good and they are bad, but both packs have done some unspeakable things. What you must understand is that this hatred between the packs has been there for many, many generations, but that we had an understanding: they leave us alone, we leave them alone. However, soon after you reached six months old, the nephew of Dark Shadow's alpha was found hanging from a tree, just over our territory line. Now, many of the pack said we should have hidden the body because it would start a war, but Jackson said the boy deserved to be buried on his homeland."

"But they believed you'd killed him?"

"Yes, and the boy's father wanted blood for the death of his son. Dark Shadow's alpha says his brother acted against his will and I believe him. The boy's father brought two of his best fighters and came onto our lands. They set a fire, cutting the rest of the pack off from your parents. By the time Jackson killed the other two men, Winter was already dying. She'd killed the boy's father, protecting you. She died in Jackson's arms that night. Jackson and many others wanted blood; they attacked Dark Shadow, and Jackson killed the alpha's mate. Slowly over the years, members of both packs have picked each other off until the pure lines are now nearly extinct and no wolf is safe outside of pack land alone."

"When will it stop? How much blood is enough?"

Karen stood up. "I don't know, Kat. I've asked myself that question many times." She left Kat alone with her thoughts and a dead weight in her stomach.

She bent her head, gripping the album in her hands as a broken sob left her. Sucking in a breath, she tried to gain control of her emotions.

Someone spoke her name, making her heart leap in her chest.

"Katalina?"

"Bass?" Katalina whispered, looking up. "Where'd you come from? I didn't hear you approach."

"Of course you didn't. I wouldn't be a very good predator if my prey heard me approach."

"Prey?" she whispered, glancing behind her to check that the house was quiet.

"I'll hear if someone comes to the door. If we're quiet, they shouldn't hear us." He cracked a smile but then it left his face. "You're crying."

She didn't bother trying to wipe her tears away; more just fell in their place anyway.

He sat down beside her. "What's wrong?"

She wasn't sure why she wanted to tell Bass. He'd called himself a predator and that word described him perfectly. She hadn't missed the fact that he'd walked onto River Run pack's land unnoticed, and she knew there were pack members out there at all times keeping watch. But it didn't seem to matter. She might be a fool for trusting him, but she did. Maybe he'd captured his prey after all, on the first night they'd met.

"I feel like I'm mourning two sets of parents, two lives. I'm so full of conflicting feelings I think I might break. My parents are dead and the life I had is never going to be the same again, and then I look at this album from my first six months of life, and I've lost the parents I had then, too. Jackson might still be alive, but the man he was . . . I think he died that night along with Winter. All that's left is a ghost clinging to a hatred that has poisoned this pack."

She sucked in a ragged breath, wiping her tears away; Bass wrapped his arm around her and she leaned into him, absorbing his heat, his steady strength. "I'm sorry. I'm sure you didn't come here to listen to my problems."

"Don't apologize, Katalina. You feel what you feel and no one can change that, but do you really want to walk away from Jackson? No matter what he's done, he is your father."

"Right now, I can't stand the sight of him, Bass. He gave me away as if I were an object he owned. He brought me here and expects me to fall in line and do as he says, when he has no right. He lost the right to have a say the night he left me on a doorstep."

They sat in silence for a while, looking out at the dark night, watching the moon travel across the sky. Content, Kat could have fallen asleep, tucked against him, warm and safe in his hold. With him, the hollowness wasn't as bad.

"Bass?" she whispered.

"Mmm?"

"Why are you here?"

She felt his laugh rumble against her side. "I already said, you intrigue me."

"That's not a real answer, Bass. Why haven't you gone home? Why would you risk being here? If they find you, they'll kill you."

"No one finds me unless I want them to, and I haven't gone home yet because I'm drawn to you."

His finger touched her chin, turning her head so that she faced him. They were just inches apart; she could feel his warm breath against her skin. Katalina's heart galloped in her chest.

*He's going to kiss me.* The thought both terrified and excited her.

Looking into his eyes, jet-black with flecks of silver, she thought was like gazing at the night sky, vast and beautiful. The corner of his mouth lifted in a slight smile. "I do quite like you, Katalina Winter. You are very intriguing and so beautiful."

Her breath caught. His hand tangled into her hair and he pulled her toward him, his smile turning wicked. He was so close. An electric force zapped between them and then his lips were on hers, and she exploded; a thousand butterflies took flight inside her. The world dropped away until she saw nothing but him, felt nothing but him.

He pulled away, looking at her with an intense hunger. "You do things to me. Make me feel things I shouldn't. I'd like to savage every member of my pack for ever thinking of hurting you. You are a dangerous temptation, Katalina Winter." His thumb rubbed over her lip, sending delicious shivers up her spine. "But then, I've always liked to play with danger."

His head shot up, a growl rumbling from his chest. "Someone is coming." He ran his lips gently over hers before leaping from the porch steps. He ran across the snow toward the trees. The second he hit their shadows, it was as if he disappeared, as if he were a shadow himself.

Katalina was still staring breathlessly at the spot where he'd vanished, wondering if he was there watching, when Cage walked outside.

"Kat? What are you doing out here? What are you looking at?"

She dragged her eyes away to look at Cage. He narrowed his eyes at the forest edge but said nothing.

"I was just coming in." She stood, feeling weak in the knees.

Cage stepped forward, steadying her. "Hey, are you okay? Your heart's racing, Kat."

"You can hear my heart?"

"Yes. Did you see something in the trees?"

"What? No. Why would you think that?"

"Well, you were staring at something and now your heart sounds like you've been running a marathon."

She pulled her arm from his. "I'm fine, honestly, but thanks for asking. I'm going to go back to bed now. Good night."

He frowned at her. "Okay. Good night, Kat."

When she closed the front door, she turned to look back outside. Cage was sniffing the air, and then he dropped his jeans, turning into a wolf, following the same path Bass had taken.

*Damn it. He'll know someone outside this pack was here.*

# CHAPTER 7

Over the next few days, Cage avoided Katalina. Toby kept her company, but there was an awkward tension between them, which made Katalina regret the words she'd said to him the other day.

"Hey, Toby?"

"Yeah?" he answered, dragging his eyes from the TV.

"We're okay, aren't we? I'm sorry about the other day."

"Of course, Kat. Tensions are a little high around here right now, but don't worry about it." He gave her a reassuring smile.

"Is Cage ever planning on talking to me again?" she asked, tucking her feet under her backside.

"He's sulking, but don't worry about it. He's fallen out with Jackson, too."

"I saw Jackson stomping around earlier. What's wrong with him?"

"I overheard Karen putting him in his place early this morning," Toby said.

"Really? I bet he hated that," she smiled.

"Sometimes it's like being surrounded by children," he said in a mock-serious tone.

Katalina started laughing just as Cage walked past the door.

He paused and backtracked. "What's so funny?" he muttered.

Toby took one look at him and fell onto the floor, laughing.

"Hilarious you are, little brother. Kat, can I have a word in private?" He crossed his arms and gave Toby a murderous look.

"Oh, um, sure." Katalina left the room, laughing at Toby. "What's up?" she asked, trying to contain her smile.

He turned and looked at her intensely. "Were you with someone the other night on the porch?"

Her heart gave a lurch. "Karen sat with me for a while. Why?"

"Someone other than one of us?"

Boom, boom, boom. Her heart pounded in her ears. "No, why? What's wrong?"

"I found a faint scent trail after you'd left."

"What?" Her heart pounded harder.

Much to her relief, Cage took her worried tone as her fearing for her life. "Kat, no one is getting near you, okay?"

"Okay . . . Have you told Jackson?" *Please say no, please say no.*

"No, I want to make sure it's really someone hanging around first. He's in such a foul mood; I'm not sure what he'll do."

"Okay." She must have looked as sick as she felt because his face softened and he lifted his hand. For a moment, she thought he was going to touch her face, but he paused halfway and squeezed her arm.

"I won't let anyone hurt you, Kat."

Katalina hated this. She hated that he cared so much and that she didn't feel the same. She hated lying to him, and most of all, she hated that he'd been brainwashed into believing it was his job to always protect her.

"Cage, you look tired. When did you last stop and eat? Come sit down and watch TV with Toby and me. It'll be fun."

He looked at the sofa longingly. "No, I'd best get back out there. I want to make sure you're safe."

"Cage, you don't need to look out for me all the time."

"I don't mind. It's my job, Kat," he answered, walking away.

"Whose job is it to look after you?" she murmured.

He paused halfway out the door and smiled sadly. "Yours if you want it."

He was gone before she could respond. She stood there feeling cold and empty, mad at the people who'd put her in this situation. She knew she shouldn't feel guilty for not doing as Jackson said, but she couldn't help it; Cage deserved better, but she had a feeling her heart had already been given away to a black-eyed wolf the night he'd found her hiding in a shed, bloody and broken.

That night, she stood at her window as she'd done the previous night, hoping and praying Bass would return. She'd stood for hours the night before, until she'd no longer been able to keep her eyes open. The urgent need she felt was silly and irrational, as if now that he was gone a piece of her was missing. She'd only known him for a very short time, yet it felt as if they'd always known each other. Every time she remembered their kiss, her heart raced and her body tingled. She was desperate for answers to the many questions that swirled in her head.

Her eyes caught movement to the left. Immediately, she froze in hope. There it was again, a movement in the shadows. Katalina left her room and quietly crept down the stairs. Faint snores carried from the front room; Cage had finally given in to his exhaustion. The front door creaked as she opened it. She paused, worried he might wake. The scrape of Arne's paws across the wooden floors made her cringe; he appeared from the kitchen, his tail wagging as he saw her.

"Come on then," she whispered. "You can be my excuse."

She closed the door and listened again but heard no one, and a quick look in the front window confirmed Cage was still fast asleep. She wrapped her arms around herself, trying to block the cold wind. Katalina stood on the porch, watching the edge of the forest, waiting to see if Bass would show himself. After what felt like an eternity, his jet-black wolf stepped from the cover of the shadows and then disappeared a second later.

Katalina ran. The snow was deep, and almost instantly she felt her injuries. She forced her sore muscles to move quickly. One look out the window and anyone in the house would see her running. Arne ran ahead of her, his head down, tail in the air as he sniffed the scents around him. He stopped when the gap between them grew too great and lapped back, his tongue hanging out in excitement.

She smiled. "Silly dog, I'm not running around for your entertainment."

She reached the trees and squinted into the dark but couldn't see anyone. Her chest heaved, dragging air into her oxygen-deprived lungs.

"Bass?" she whispered, taking a few more steps into the woods. She could only see a short distance and not very well. She moved slowly, arms outstretched so as not to face-plant into a tree.

"Bass!" she called a little louder, her heart pounding. *What if it wasn't Bass at all?* "Bass, where are you?"

Arne stepped in front of her, growling. She saw his eyes first, just silver flecks like stars in the night sky, and then the outline of his large wolf. He was so dark he was almost invisible. He looked up at Katalina and then at Arne. Bass growled back and Arne instantly silenced.

"Hey! Leave him alone. He's just protecting me from the big bad wolf," she laughed.

His wolf padded farther into the woods as Katalina followed.

"Bass, slow down. I can barely see you!" she whispered. Her foot was aching something awful and she was beginning to wish he'd come to her.

"Bass?" She'd lost sight of him. Peering into the darkness, feeling disoriented, she called again, "Bass, where are you?"

"Big bad wolf, am I?" he murmured, appearing before her.

Gasping, Katalina jumped. It was as if he'd appeared out of nowhere. He chuckled at her. "Sorry. Did I scare you?"

"Yes! How do you do that?"

"Do what?"

"Just appear? I didn't hear you or see you until you were in my face."

"Partly because I'm a wolf, partly because I'm good at blending into the shadows. I told you. No one sees me unless I want to be seen."

"Hmm." Katalina had just noticed his bare chest and the tattered-looking pair of jeans hanging low on his waist; he wore nothing else. Immediately, she couldn't pull together a single coherent sentence. She imagined what it would feel like running her hands over each ridge of his abs.

"You're staring, Kat."

"What?"

"I said you are staring." He reached out his hand and tilted her chin up. She stared into his amused eyes.

"How long have you had those jeans on?" she asked, seeing how dirty they were.

"Well, not that long considering I'm a wolf most of the time, but being carried around by a wolf and dumped on the ground isn't the best for keeping clothes clean." He stepped closer, his bare skin just inches from her. "Am I too dirty for you, Katalina Winter?"

She gulped, feeling like slapping the smirk from his face. She stepped back, needing room to think of anything other than his body. *Get a grip, Kat. He's only kissed you once!*

"You didn't come last night."

"No. The wolf who interrupted us, he tracked me after I left. He's very good. Fortunately, I'm better. He has been very persistent in his goal to catch me. Coming to you would have been too great a risk. I saw you waiting, though."

"You did?"

"Yes, you stood at the window for a long time."

"Yes," she answered, casting her eyes down in embarrassment.

"I like that you waited."

She snapped her head up. "You do?"

He chuckled again, amusement dancing in his eyes.

*God, could you sound any lamer, Kat?*

He stepped forward, his arm wrapping around her waist. Her breath left her in a rush as he pulled her against himself. "I do," he breathed into her mouth, kissing her softly.

Katalina moaned as she melted against him. She looked at him breathlessly, all the questions she'd wanted to ask buried under her desire.

"Did you miss me?" he asked her quietly.

For a moment, she wondered whether to tell him the truth. What would he think? They'd only known each other for a short time, but in that short time, he'd consumed her. She'd thought of nothing else the previous night, and when he didn't turn up, her heart had ached.

"Yes," she said quietly, looking at the ground again.

"Good." He met her lips again; his hands ran slowly up her back and into her hair.

She shivered, her whole body alive from his touch. His tongue dipped into her mouth, making her knees weaken. Running her hands up his back, she gripped him tighter, his skin like fire under her fingertips.

Bass pulled away from her, breathing heavily. Smiling, Katalina felt pleased it wasn't just her so affected.

"As much as I'd love to kiss you all night, I need to tell you something, Kat," he said, the tone of his voice suddenly going from playful to serious.

She instantly felt cold. "About what?"

"Hey, don't worry. It's not that bad. Well, I hope you don't think it's that bad. I just—I needed to tell you before this went any further."

"Okay," she whispered, feeling even more worried by his rambling. Bass had never rambled before.

"I'm from Dark Shadow. I told you that, and that a lot of my pack wants you dead—well, my father . . ."

"Bass, I already know this and no doubt, your father wants me dead. Your father would have to do as he's told."

"No, Kat, you don't understand. My full name is Sebastian Evernight. My father is the alpha."

Her heart was racing. If Bass was the son of Dark Shadow's alpha, then that meant Jackson had killed his mother. Katalina felt sick. How could he not want her dead?

"Kat, please, I do not care what my father thinks, so it doesn't matter."

"How can you say that, when Jackson killed your mother? God, Bass, how can you even look at me?"

Bass ran his finger along her jaw. "Katalina, Dark Shadow is responsible for the death of your parents and the death of Winter, yet you look at me with a warmth in your eyes that makes me feel whole. Both of our packs are responsible for so much death. This all started when we had no control over the situation, but now I can put a stop to the bloodshed. It is time the past is left where it belongs."

"But why, Bass? Why would you go against your father for me?"

Bass smiled at her, taking her face in his hands. "Haven't you figured it out yet?" He lightly brushed his lips over hers. "There is something between us, Katalina; something not even eighteen years of hatred can destroy."

He let go of her face, resting his hands on her hips. It was Katalina who closed the distance between them. She wrapped her arms around him tightly, feeling truly happy for the first time since the night of her eighteenth birthday. They kissed with a hunger, a passion that made the rest of the world drop away. For the seconds she held him, Katalina didn't feel anything but Bass. His heat caressed her as she ran her hands over bare skin. His steady strength and the taste of him on her tongue consumed her every sense.

The feelings Katalina felt for Bass had developed with a speed she didn't understand. Their intensity frightened her at times, yet when she was with him, some of the sadness disappeared. He made her feel as if she could cope with the loss in her life. She didn't understand it, but it was simply right.

Arne barked from somewhere in the distance, and Katalina jumped. She'd completely forgotten he'd come with her.

"Arne! Come here," Katalina called quietly. Moments later, he dashed out of the trees, wrapping himself around her legs.

"Thanks for the interruption, dog," Bass grumbled.

Katalina laughed at him. "I best be getting back. Cage was asleep on the sofa when I snuck out."

"This Cage. I do not like the way he watches you."

"How do you know how he looks at me? Have you been spying?"

"I did tell you I was good at blending in, didn't I?"

"Jackson promised me to Cage."

Bass growled.

"Hey, leave Cage alone, okay? He's a nice guy. It's not his fault Jackson is an ass." The look of displeasure left Bass's face as quickly as it arrived. Katalina expected Bass to comment further on the subject of Cage, the hard set of his mouth telling her he wasn't happy being told to leave Cage alone. Yet he looked at her intensely. It was as if he could read her soul. A look of satisfaction crossed his face before he moved on.

"Katalina, I won't be here for the next few days. I need to go back home. If I don't return soon, my father will send someone looking for me."

"What are you going to say to him? Will you tell him about us?"

"I'm not sure. My father may not take the news too well, and I want to be back before the full moon," he answered uncertainly, a frown line marking his forehead. "My father can be very difficult," he continued sadly.

At the mention of the full moon, Katalina felt her stomach turn. She'd been trying very hard not to think about what would happen when that day came.

"Don't worry, Kat. I won't let you go through it alone. Being a wolf is the most incredible feeling. You'll see. I promise."

He knew exactly what to say to ease her mounting worry. She did not understand the connection they had, yet his reassurance and soothing words were exactly what Katalina needed to hear. With a resigned sigh, she knew it was time to go. "Okay, I best go." She kissed him again, wishing he didn't have to hide in the woods. "Come on, Arne. Time to go." Bass kissed her forehead before she turned to leave.

After a few steps, Katalina realized she'd be unable to run back to the house. Although her leg was healing well, she knew she shouldn't have been going so far on it.

Bass was suddenly beside her. "Kat, your leg—why didn't you tell me? I should have never let you walk here. I'm not used to being around people who do not heal almost instantly." He picked her up.

"Bass, Cage could be watching." Her heart stuttered at their closeness and his strong arms cradling her body.

"Let him watch. I won't have you damaging yourself further." She didn't have time to protest; he started to run, Arne following.

He carried her as if she weighed nothing. When he reached the house, he wasn't the least bit out of breath. Bass kissed her before standing her upright. "Good night, Katalina."

She watched him run back to the trees and melt into the shadows.

"Come on, boy. It's time for bed," she said, opening the front door with a smile.

That night, Katalina had no trouble falling asleep. Bass filled her dreams, keeping the burning nightmares at bay.

# CHAPTER 8

Cage went from completely ignoring Katalina to never leaving her side. She knew it had to do with Bass; not that Cage knew that. All he knew was there were strange scent trails in the surrounding woods and he'd smelled them near her. He had no real evidence she'd been with Bass, but he was planning on finding some.

She hated him constantly watching her. Every move she made, he watched. Toby noticed, too; she'd overheard them arguing. Toby seemed to think his brother had lost his bearings. He'd tried talking to Katalina about it, but Cage had found them before he'd had the chance.

Normally, Katalina wouldn't have minded Cage's company. He'd been happy and caring since she'd first met him. Now he seemed edgy; he crowded her and snapped easily. He was finally cracking under the expectations put on him at far too young an age.

It was the night before the full moon when he finally found some evidence. The night sky was clear and the almost-full moon bright. Sneaking the first bit of alone time she'd had in days, she went outside, wrapped in a blanket. Arne scrambled about in the snow, running back to Katalina on the porch steps every so often. The peace was wonderful, and she felt herself relaxing for the first time since Bass had left. But her peace was shattered when the front door opened; Cage joined her on the steps, his suspicious eyes scanning the woods.

"Kat, what are you doing?" he demanded.

"I was enjoying some alone time," she answered in the same harsh tone he'd used.

"I've told you, someone is out there. Get inside. It's not safe!"

She chose to ignore him. If he was going to talk to her like she were a child, she'd act like one. She knew it wasn't the best plan, but it was the only one she had.

"Kat, I said *inside*!" He pointed to the door and Katalina laughed. "I'm serious!"

"Really? I couldn't tell." She continued watching Arne.

When she didn't move, Cage walked the two steps between them and roughly dragged Katalina to her feet. Arne's head snapped up and he gave a warning growl.

"Cage, get off me! What makes you think you have the right to treat me like this?"

"I'm protecting you!"

"How is hurting me, protecting me? The way you've been lately, I'll be pleased when I never have to spend a minute with you again!" Kat shouted, pulling away from him; the blanket around her slipped to the porch floor.

The anger suddenly left him and a look of horror crossed his face. "You're right." He bent to pick up her blanket. "I'm sorry—" He stopped midsentence and brought the blanket to his face, breathing deeply.

The anger returned to his face. His body trembled with rage as he towered over her. Arne, sensing Cage's sudden mood change, jumped up onto the porch and pushed himself between them.

"Who is he, Kat?" Cage growled at her.

"Who?" Katalina worked hard to keep the fear out of her voice.

"The fucking guy whose scent is on this blanket!"

Arne snapped at Cage's legs, growling and barking a loud warning. Cage took a step back but didn't seem at all bothered.

"Cage, you are being ridiculous. I have no idea what you're talking about."

"I can smell the lie, Kat, and I can smell him on here." He thrust the blanket at her, making her stumble back. "I'm not stupid, Kat. You've been seeing someone and you are going to tell me who he is. Now!"

For the first time since she'd met Cage, she felt frightened; her heart stuttered, eyes widening as she looked at him. Eyes lit with rage, jaw clenched, and hands balled tightly, he seemed capable of hurting her. She wondered what he'd do if she shouted for help. As if reading her mind, he took a step to the side, blocking her way back inside. Through his clenched jaw, he said, "Don't even think of shouting, Kat. I'm a lot quicker than you."

"Do you know what, Cage? When I first met you, I actually thought we could be friends, but I can see now that's never going to happen, not with the way you are acting. If you must know, yes, I have being seeing someone, but I'm not telling you who he is." Katalina squared her shoulders, her gaze daring him to shout.

His clenched fist snatched at her shirt, dragging her forward so he was inches from her face. "You'll tell me now, Kat. Who is he? Is he from this pack?"

Arne was barking loudly, but Cage didn't even seem to notice him. Kat attempted to push her fear aside, despite her pounding heart, but she couldn't help the small tremble as she whispered her answer, "N-no, he's Dark Sh-shadow."

The front door opened.

"Cage!" Jackson growled, his tone pure alpha.

Cage had no choice but to release Katalina, but it did nothing to dull the fury raging through his veins.

"What do you think you're doing?" Jackson shouted, dragging Cage away from Katalina.

Katalina ran her hand through her hair and straightened her clothes. She pulled the blanket back around her, half covering her face, and she drew Bass's scent into her lungs, wrapping him around her.

"She's seeing someone from Dark Shadow. His scent is all over the pack woods!" Cage yelled, dragging himself from Jackson's grip.

Jackson glanced at Cage, then at Katalina. "Kat?"

Katalina simply nodded.

"Are you insane? The Dark Shadow pack wants you dead."

"Not all of them," she answered quietly.

"Katalina, they cannot be trusted! You are not to see him again!"

Katalina's temper snapped. She stood up straight, staring Jackson right in the eyes, not caring in the slightest that he was an alpha and demanded respect.

"You have no idea whether he can be trusted or not! From what I know, he's far more trustworthy than any of you! You have no right to tell me what to do, *Jackson*!"

"I'm your father."

"You don't know the first thing about being a father," Katalina scoffed.

"I'm the alpha."

Katalina stormed past them and headed back inside, Arne on her heels.

"Not *my* alpha!" she shouted as she went up the stairs.

Katalina slammed the door to the bedroom, which was feeling more like a prison by the minute. She wished she were with Bass. Things were better when he was near. She heard shouting downstairs, but had given up caring what anyone in this house had to say. Pulling the blanket around her, she crawled into bed, while Arne curled up on the floor, his eyes ever watchful.

"Don't worry, boy. We just have to get through the full moon, and then we are outta here!"

*****

The full moon arrived. Katalina paced her room, feeling restless and trapped, wanting nothing more than to get out of the house. She hadn't left the bedroom since the previous night, and no one had come to her after the argument.

A door slammed downstairs, making Katalina pause and listen.

"I've picked up his scent all over the woods, right up to the house. Jack ran the perimeter. He's been coming across territory lines near the ridge, but I couldn't find him. He's either left or is very good at hiding."

"Damn it! She'll be most vulnerable tonight. Everyone who is of age to fight needs to be out there now looking for him!" Jackson ordered.

Katalina's stomach gave a lurch. She hoped Bass could reach her without being caught.

"But what about Katalina? She'll change soon," Cage said.

"Well, she'll just have to change in the house!"

"What? You can't be serious. It's hard enough the first time without being trapped in a room."

"Do you have a better idea?" Jackson snapped.

"We're not even sure he is out there anymore. I picked up only one scent and it wasn't fresh. If we all go out and protect her, she can change in the open and run with the pack. She'll be protected and it will make the transition easier."

"No, absolutely not. It's too dangerous. Now get out there, Cage. You're one of our best fighters and the best tracker in the pack."

"I'm not leaving her. She needs someone to help her change."

*I don't want you anywhere near me, after the way you acted last night.* She hoped to God Jackson would send him away.

"Out—now, Cage! That's a direct order. You can help her by killing whoever is out there."

"Jackson, he does have a point. Someone needs to be with the girl, someone she trusts," Karen added.

"Well, they're not exactly friends after what he did last night. TOBY!"

"Um, yes, I didn't hear—"

"I don't care if you were listening in. You're to stay and protect Katalina. Help her change, understand?"

"Yes, sir, you can count on me."

*Great. How am I going to get past Toby?*

"Good. See, Cage, all sorted. Now get out there and hunt!"

Katalina moved away from the door as she heard Toby's feet shuffling up the stairs. She didn't want a babysitter and she wasn't in the mood to see Toby. He was always so happy and full of life. She felt like ripping someone apart, not making happy chitchat. The thought of changing into a wolf terrified her. She knew Toby only wanted to help, but somewhere out there, Bass was waiting. Her instinct told her to go to Bass, and to do that she needed to be alone.

"Kat?" Toby called, knocking on the door.

"Yeah?"

His head appeared around the door. "Hey, how's things?" he asked, smiling.

"I know what's going on, Toby. You're not the only one who can eavesdrop."

"Hey! I wasn't listening. I happened to walk up to the door and thought it would be rude to just walk in."

Katalina couldn't help but laugh at the innocent expression on his face. "Okay, Toby, but I'm fine. I just wanna be alone, okay?"

"All right, Kat, but shout if you need me, or if you think you're gonna change, okay?"

"Yep," she said, smiling too brightly. He left anyway, a frown marring his normally happy face.

As soon as he shut the door, Katalina pulled off her woolen sweater. Her temperature was rising. Arne whined at her. "Shush, boy, I'm just hot is all. I'm going to be fine. Bass is going to come and we are going to go home."

But as the moon rose farther into the sky, Katalina began to feel anything but fine. Her skin itched; she couldn't stop scratching. She scratched until she bled. Pulling her shoes and socks off, she tried to cool herself down but nothing worked. Walking out of the room, she locked herself in the bathroom and threw water over her face. Bracing her hands on the sink, looking at herself in the mirror, flushed red, she looked like she had a fever, and her silky hair was matted with sweat.

A small part of her wanted to call Toby for help, but another part of her refused. She liked Toby and she did trust him, but he was part of River Run, a part of Jackson's pack. Accepting Toby's help felt like giving in to Jackson's demands. She didn't need Jackson, she didn't need River Run; to admit that they were a part of her was to admit Jackson was her father, and she didn't want him as a father—she already had one.

"God, what's happening to me?"

Her stomach suddenly lurched. She fell onto the floor, gripping at her middle, biting back a groan.

"Kat, are you all right?" Toby asked, knocking.

"Yes, Toby, please go back downstairs," she forced out through clenched teeth.

"Are you sure? Maybe I should come in?"

"No, Toby. Honestly, I'm fine."

"All right. Cage just called. They've not found anyone yet."

"Right." *Bass* . . .

"Shout if you need me!" he called, bounding down the stairs.

"Ugh!" Katalina threw up. She retched, trying her best to be quiet, until there was nothing but bile in her stomach and her throat burned from the acid.

Pulling off another layer of clothing, she rubbed at her skin; it felt tight. Her neck bled where she'd scratched it raw. She needed to get outside; the house was too small. There wasn't enough air. Pulling the window up, Katalina lowered herself down. Digging her fingers into the boards, she scaled down the side of the house. A ripple of pain traveled up her spine. Crying out, she fell to the ground. Moaning, she rolled over, noticing the snow melting beneath her burning skin. Standing, Katalina ran for the forest edge, but more pain shot through her. She bit down on her lip, tasting blood, trying her hardest not to cry out in pain. The last thing she wanted was the pack to find her.

She heard distant calls and knew she needed to get away.

Half crawling, half running, she made it into the trees as another wave of pain washed over her. She retched again, this time crying out as the pain became too much. Her hands stretched and cracked; her body was breaking apart from the inside.

"Arrh!" she screamed, stumbling farther into the forest, colliding with trees, not noticing the bark grazing her skin or the fallen branches cutting at her feet.

Another wave of agony and she half changed. Her feet became wolf paws, her nails changed into deadly, sharp claws. Pulling her jeans off, Katalina crawled over the ground, tears rolling down her face, mixing with the sweat coating her skin. Her heart boomed in her ears, each pulse throbbing inside her skull.

Fear was thick on her tongue, coating her throat and stealing her breath. She'd never felt anything like it.

She screamed again, panting hard, trying to suck oxygen into her body.

*Bass . . . Bass . . . I need Bass.*

She screamed his name in between each ripple of pain, each cracking of bones. "BASS!" she yelled again, not caring who else heard her.

"Please, Bass," she sobbed, searching the trees. She didn't know how she knew, but she knew he was out there somewhere, searching for her. "BASS!"

He darted through the trees, invisible but for the few silver flecks in his eyes, and seeing him calmed her racing heart.

He changed, kneeling down in front of her. "Katalina, shush, there are others out here."

"Bass, make it stop. Please, make it stop," she sobbed, clinging to him. "I can't."

She screamed, hands turning into paws. "Bass, please," she begged, gasping for breath through the never-ending pain.

"Katalina, stop fighting it. This is who you are. Let your wolf out." He rubbed her back and murmured, "Let it out, Kat."

"I don't know how. Please, Bass, I'm so scared. Help me . . . arrh . . . !"

"Kat, Katalina, look at me. Look into my eyes." He tilted her chin up and she stared at his dark, dark eyes. "Breathe, Kat. Breathe with me." Holding his gaze, she tried to match his breaths. She desperately tried to relax as the pain rocked through her. "That's it, Katalina. This is who you are. You are a wolf, Katalina Winter. Let her out."

As he whispered those words to her, a final rush of pain rippled through her and then she was a wolf. Bass smiled at her, his head coming level with hers. "Katalina, you are a beautiful wolf."

Unsteady on her legs, she looked down at her paws; they were as white as the snow blanketing the forest. She turned her head to see thick white fur.

"Run with me," Bass whispered against her head, running his hands through her coat, making her shiver with pleasure. "Run with me." Bass turned and jumped, changing into his wolf midair.

Taking a tentative step forward, she realized it felt as natural as walking when human. Bass rubbed his head against her side. She could sense his urgency to go, his black coat in stark contrast to her white as they ran through the woods, away from the pack.

She'd never felt so free, with the wind whipping past her and the ground flying beneath her fast, agile paws. Bass ran with her, running around her, jumping over her. The silver flecks in his eyes sparkled with joy. She ran until she couldn't run anymore. Collapsing, she changed back, too exhausted to feel self-conscious about being naked, smiling at the black wolf as he licked her face. "Hey!" she laughed as he changed.

"Come, Katalina, it's time for you to go home," he murmured, lifting her into his arms.

She nestled her head against his bare chest, feeling safe in the arms of the boy she'd come to trust. The rightness of his cradling arms subdued her need for him, a need somewhat similar to breathing.

He carried her through the woods. Exhaustion swept through her, her body aching. "Bass, I feel terrible."

"You will for a few hours. It fades with each change."

Her eyes slid shut.

"Kat?" he murmured against her ear, rousing her.

"Hmm?"

"It's time I leave." The tone of his voice made Katalina snap to alert. She looked at the house across from them. Several members of River Run were hanging around.

"They've not sensed us yet, but they will shortly." As the words left his mouth, she saw someone look right at them and shout to Jackson.

Bass put her down. She wrapped her arms around herself tightly. Cage started to run toward them, a look of pure fury on his face, and others followed.

"Bass?" Katalina gasped, frightened.

He kissed her gently. "Don't worry about me. Be ready to leave at first dark. I will come for you."

Bass took off into the trees, changing as he ran. Cage raced past her a second later, the others following him. She didn't know what to do or say; she felt too weak to protest. She just hoped Bass was as good as he said.

"Kat?"

Katalina turned toward Toby's voice as he offered her a blanket. She'd barely registered the cold seeping into her bare skin.

"I thought you'd need this. Are you feeling okay? The first change can be rough."

"Thanks, Toby." She smiled, covering her naked body with the blanket. "I'm just tired and so hungry."

"Come on." He wrapped his arm around her and helped her into the house. Katalina stopped off at the kitchen for food and then went to the bedroom. As she climbed onto the bed, she called out to Toby as he was closing the door.

"Toby."

"Yeah?"

"Thank you."

"For what?"

"For always being there, for not judging me."

"It's all right, Kat."

"I'm going to miss you," she whispered as he closed the door.

She couldn't be certain, but she thought he whispered back, "I'll miss you too, Kat."

# CHAPTER 9

With a full belly, Katalina fell instantly into a deep sleep. She woke up at midday, her stomach growling as she climbed out of bed.

*God, I'm starving.*

She turned the handle, intending to go find food, but the door was locked. Katalina rattled the handle and then banged against the door. Her heart pounded. *They've locked me in.* She'd felt like a prisoner from the moment she'd arrived, but in that instant, she really was. She banged again and started shouting.

Jackson's voice drifted through the door a moment later.

"This is for your own good, Katalina. As soon as that wolf is caught, you'll be free to leave your room."

She felt sick, her head fuzzy. Each pound of her heart boomed through her skull. She had to be careful; she needed to make them think she'd behave or she'd never get away.

"Jackson, please. I won't leave the house. I'm hungry and bored," she said in her sweetest voice.

"I'll send Toby up with food. Sorry, Kat, you're staying put."

A surge of anger raced through her and then a sharp pain spread through her fingers. She gasped at the hand she had pressed against the door. Changing and cracking, it morphed into a wolf's paw. With great effort, Katalina managed to regain control of her body and keep her wolf at bay, but she knew only the smallest thing would set it off again.

*Oh my God, what has happened to me?* Anger consumed her.

She paced the room, feeling more agitated by the second. Her body didn't feel like her own anymore. There was a rage, a wildness inside of her and it scared Katalina. Glancing out of the window, she realized Bass would come for her in a few hours. She needed to get out of the room. *I need to go home.*

The door clicked and then opened. Toby looked miserable when he walked in carrying a tray of food.

*Sorry,* he mouthed. The door closed behind him and clicked, locking Toby inside with her.

Katalina sat in silence eating the food, racking her brain for some semblance of a plan, or at least some idea of how to escape. She could barge past when they let Toby out, or climb out the window when he left. She stood and walked over to the window. Cage was circling the house, keeping her in and Bass out. *Can I get past Cage?*

She watched him as he vanished from view, lapping around the back; it took him two minutes to come back around the front. Two minutes she'd have to climb out the window and make it to the cover of the woods. She wasn't even sure she could do that with her new wolf speed.

"He nailed the window shut while you were sleeping, Kat," Toby whispered.

Katalina turned and looked at Toby with wide eyes. "While I was sleeping? Are you for real?"

"The body takes the first change hard. I slept for more than twenty-four hours after mine. There could have been a riot outside and you wouldn't have noticed." His voice was a gravelly whisper.

"What is my best chance of escape, Toby?" she whispered.

Toby looked at the door, the window, and then back at Katalina. Taking a deep breath, he whispered, "If I can slip away, I'll open the door. You'll have to then sneak out, wait for Cage to be out of sight, and run. I'm not even sure if I'll be able to get the door unlocked, and then you've got to get through the house and past Cage. Kat, it's going to be pretty hard. The best chance you'll have is turning wolf. You'll be quicker. Jackson has all four enforcers patrolling around the pack's perimeter, too. He'll come after you straight away. You'll have to keep running and pray you can get enough of a head start to outrun them."

"You'd do that for me?"

"It's only unlocking a door."

"No, Toby, it's going against your alpha to help me."

"This isn't right, Kat. I can't just sit back and do nothing. Cage has gone insane. I've no idea why he's siding with Jackson."

There was a bang on the door. "Toby, time to come out."

"See you, Kat," Toby smiled.

Katalina spent the next hour pacing. She'd given up trying to open the window; it was well and truly nailed shut. She'd watched Cage for a while; his constant marching drove her mad. Arne was still running around free, which made her feel better, but she wasn't sure she'd be able to sneak out and get his attention.

She froze as the door clicked softly. Rushing to the door, Katalina listened for any sounds and when she heard nothing, she crept out. It was time. When she was halfway down the stairs, the front door opened. Karen rushed in, slamming it so hard behind her that the glass in the tiny rectangular window cracked. Katalina stood frozen, her heart in her throat, but Karen didn't notice her as she marched into the kitchen. Jackson started shouting and then Karen started shouting back. For a second, Katalina didn't move. She'd never heard Karen so mad, but then she realized her advantage: their fighting would distract them as she escaped.

Hurrying down the last few steps, Katalina waited until Cage was out of sight and then ran. Luckily, Arne was asleep on the porch. The second she leaped off the front steps, he woke and ran after her. Halfway to the woods she remembered that Toby told her to change. Having only done it once—and without wanting to that first time—now she wasn't sure what to do. Pulling her clothes off as she ran, she tripped, landing face-first in the snow.

"Fuck it!" she swore, dragging her jeans off and then jumping back to her feet. As she started to run again, she heard Cage yell.

"Here goes nothing," she muttered.

Katalina closed her eyes. She pictured her wolf in her mind's eye, instinctively knowing this was how to take control of her wolf. The pain of the change ran up her spine. She screamed, falling forward as her wolf burst from within her.

Cage had already closed the distance between them, but she didn't look back. The woods became a different world as a wolf. She could see and feel the best path through the trees. Her paws easily glided over the uneven earth, but Cage had been a wolf longer than she had and he was soon snapping at her heels.

Arne was already far behind them, not able to keep up with the wolves, but she couldn't think of him now; she had to think of herself, no matter how much it hurt her to leave him behind.

Cage jumped onto her. They tumbled to the ground, a ball of snow-white and dark-gray fur. Katalina was startled by the savage snarl that ripped from her throat. She leapt to her feet, prowling around him, her wolf instincts taking over. Cage snarled back at her. He was twice as big and more muscular. His growl vibrated through her bones, and she felt the command in his tone. He was more dominant than she was, higher in rank within the pack, but Katalina didn't truly belong to the pack. She shook off the command, leaped toward him, and sunk her sharp wolf teeth into his flank.

Cage had spent his whole life training to fight. He'd been a wolf for many years and Katalina was no match for him. He had her pinned within a matter of minutes. He snarled above her, snapping at her exposed throat. Ice-cold fear flooded her veins, causing her human form to come through.

Cage changed back. "Well done, Kat. I'm impressed. You've been a wolf one night and you actually managed to draw blood." He smiled at her as if it was all some big game. "Imagine how powerful you'll be when I've trained you."

"You'll never train me, Cage. I'm not staying here!" she spat at him. Lashing out, her nails scratched against skin, drawing blood.

Anger flared in his eyes, but he didn't fight back. "Back home," he snapped.

Cage lifted her up, his arm tight around her waist as he dragged her back to the house. Katalina didn't go quietly; she kicked and screamed, slashing her nails across his skin, but he didn't let her go.

"That's not my home! It will never be my home. Put me down!" she screamed.

"For God's sake, Kat, will you just stop? Do you think I want to be doing this? Dark Shadow wants you dead and they're responsible for your parents' deaths. I can't let that happen, can't let them hurt you. This is for your own good. Please just stop fighting. We're supposed to be friends, remember?"

Katalina went slack in his arms. Cage let her go as she relaxed, realizing she'd given up trying to escape. She fell back, her naked ass hitting the snow.

"Friends! If you were my friend, you'd be taking me back to my home, so I can say good-bye to my parents. We could have been friends once, but not anymore." Kat jumped to her feet, turned on her heel, and stormed back to the house, collecting her discarded clothes along the way.

"Kat!" Jackson growled at her as she walked up the porch steps.

"I want to go home, Jackson!"

"This is your home," he said, barely containing his fury.

"No, it isn't. If this were my home, I'd be free to come and go as I pleased. This is my prison. You claim to be my father, but fathers don't lock up their daughters."

"I'm sorry, Katalina, but this is for your own good."

"I'm sorry, too."

He looked at her, surprise etched on his face at her apology.

Katalina's jaw clenched tightly, her body rigid with anger. She slapped Jackson across the face, the force jarring her arm. Everyone gasped as the slap echoed around them.

"I've never hated someone so much in my life!" she growled.

Cage grabbed her before she could launch herself at Jackson. She screamed all the way up the stairs, gouging her fingernails into his back. Cage flung her to the floor, slamming the door shut and locking her in.

Climbing to her feet, she trembled with an anger she'd never felt before. It swirled and grew inside her like a tornado, ripping from her in a savage scream. She lunged at the door, and her shoulder connected and smashed through the wood. Splinters exploded around her as she traveled through and landed in a heap on the other side.

She heaved in a breath, trying to gain some control, but nothing would calm the storm inside her. Her wolf paced, pushing against her skin, straining to escape. Pain rippled down her spine, her claws gouged into the wooden boards beneath her; her wolf fought for its freedom and won.

She prowled forward on wolf paws, a growl rumbling through her chest. She couldn't think beyond the red haze of anger. Katalina pounced on the nearest person she found. Blood filled her mouth as her sharp wolf teeth tore into flesh. *Toby's flesh . . . Toby's blood . . .*

The red haze dropped as ice ran through her veins, forcing the change. Toby lay bleeding in her arms.

"Oh God, what have I done?" she sobbed.

"Kat," Toby croaked.

"Toby, Toby, I'm so sorry. I . . . I don't know what . . . I was so angry . . . I . . . please, please be okay."

"Katalina!" Jackson pushed her away, lifting Toby into his arms. "Just go! Go back to your room!"

Katalina ran back to her room without complaint. She slumped to the floor naked, staring at the blood staining her hands, wondering how she'd become such a monster. Time passed but she didn't seem to notice. All she could think of was Toby—young, sweet Toby, covered in blood, because of her.

Sometime later, she noticed a guard outside her room. The broken pieces of door remained scattered all around, reminding her of the strength she now possessed, the power that she couldn't contain. She climbed to her feet, her body protesting from sitting in one position for so long. She pulled on the nearest clothes she could find and walked to the man guarding her door.

"Can I go wash my hands?" she asked in a small voice. She didn't recognize him. He hadn't been in the house before. He looked at her, his brown eyes hard with anger.

"No!"

The man was broad shouldered, his body covered in muscle. Katalina turned away from the door, not daring to protest.

She heard whining outside. Going to the window, she saw Arne. No one seemed to be letting him in. "Looks like we are both in trouble," she whispered against the glass, pressing her hand on the cold surface. She longed for freedom, for home.

"Kat?"

Katalina whipped around. Was he a hallucination? How was he on his feet so fast?

"You're okay?" she asked quietly, not daring to move in case he wasn't real. She'd honestly thought she'd killed him, after seeing all the blood that had covered her. Yet there he stood, bandaged and looking a little pale, but alive. She'd never been so happy to see him.

"Yes, takes more than a bite to put me down. I'll be right as rain by morning."

"But the b-blood?" she stammered, looking at her red-stained hands.

Toby followed her eyes and frowned. "Why haven't you cleaned up?"

Katalina glanced toward the door. "He wouldn't let me out. Best to keep the monster locked away."

"Kat!" Toby took a step toward her. "You are not a monster. Do you hear me? None of this is your fault, none. You're a newly changed wolf who hasn't had any guidance. Jackson has kept you locked up like a prisoner. I'm surprised you've kept it together this long. Being a shifter is amazing, but it also comes with problems. Part of you is a wild animal, and sometimes that animal takes over."

"I don't want this, Toby." Katalina shook her head, close to tears. She was about to say more when she felt a strange pull in her chest. Turning, she looked out the window with a frown.

"What is it, Kat?" Toby asked.

Katalina looked over her shoulder at him. "I-I'm not sure."

There it was again, a pull in her chest, a sense that someone was calling to her. The sun was setting. *Bass . . .*

"Kat?" Toby said, sterner.

*He's here. Bass has come for me . . .*

Katalina felt time slow as her brain worked a mile a minute. She needed to escape, but her door was guarded and Jackson was downstairs. *Cage—where's Cage?*

"Toby, where's Cage?"

"Jackson sent him home. Said his presence was winding up your wolf."

"So no one is guarding the house? Who's here?"

"No . . . Kat, what's going on? You're safe. Jackson is here and Ned is an enforcer." He nodded toward the door.

*Just Jackson and an enforcer to get past.*

She saw a truck in the far distance.

Katalina picked up a vase and smiled at Toby, sending him a look of apology in the process. She threw the vase. It smashed loudly against the window, cracking the glass. The sound of Jackson's feet running for the stairs urged her to move. Leaping, Katalina smashed through the window. She landed on her side in the snow, wishing she had more control over her wolf so she could have changed and landed on her paws. The impact knocked the air from her lungs. Stunned, she was unable to breathe as her nerves pulsed with pain. Sucking in a gravelly breath, she pushed up with her arms, blood dripping onto the snow, its stark crimson leaving its mark on the pristine earth.

Shouts from inside the house brought her body back to life. She leapt to her feet, running for the truck that had travelled past the forest edge. Katalina was surprised no bones had been broken from the fall. Her feet glided across the ground, fast and sure. A quick glance over her shoulder confirmed Arne was following, and Jackson had just burst through the front door.

"Katalina!" His voice echoed all around her, the power in it vibrating through her bones. She shook it off, pushing her legs faster, moving toward Bass. He'd just spun the truck around and headed back toward the trees.

"Katalina, I order you to stop, as your alpha!" His voice reverberated through her, causing her steps to falter. She felt her wolf rise to the surface, brushing against her skin, wanting out.

She could feel it, the natural instinct to change; her wolf was stronger and faster, and she needed to escape. Katalina forced herself to relax to let her wolf through. When an image of Toby entered her mind, the feel of his warm blood filling her mouth, she gasped, forcing the wolf back.

"I'm your alpha. Obey me!"

He was right behind her. She could almost feel his fingers brushing against her. Arne ran at her side. The command rolled through her again. *No! You're not my alpha. You are no one to me!*

Katalina found more strength within her, pushing herself faster. The truck ground to a stop. Bass climbed partway out, his eyes frantic.

But Jackson was an alpha—though he couldn't command her, he still had the strength and speed of an alpha, which Katalina didn't possess. His fingers brushed her skin and she heard a growl rumble from his human throat.

"Go!" she yelled at Bass. The truck started moving; it was just a yard away.

Katalina pushed off the ground, stretching as she jumped. Her upper body landed in the back of the moving vehicle. Her hands scrambled for something to hold onto, wrapping around a bar as Jackson took hold of her ankle. The truck was now speeding away, swerving from side to side, trying to loosen Jackson, but his hand only tightened around her.

"Let go!" he growled.

Katalina gripped the bar with all her strength as she half turned her body. She looked into Jackson's angry eyes. "Let me go!" she screamed, kicking her free foot into his face.

Arne was still running after the truck, but he wasn't quick enough to make the jump.

"Bass, Arne!" she yelled, kicking out again in hopes of making Jackson let go.

The truck suddenly braked, causing Jackson to collide with the back; Arne jumped, his legs scrambling on the smooth metal as he landed beside Katalina; her arm jarred, stretching painfully as Bass put his foot back on the accelerator. Gravel sprayed up as the tires skidded, making Jackson lose his footing. Katalina screamed as Jackson's weight pulled against her.

"Let me go, Jackson!" she yelled. She was losing her grip, unable to take his full weight.

He was dragging behind the truck, his feet scrambling for grip. Determination flooded Katalina as her foot connected with his nose. His blood splattered against her bare feet. Her hold was slipping; she was going to fall. Fear of being trapped in that house forever coursed through her. At that moment, Arne leapt forward, sinking his teeth into Jackson's wrist. Jackson yelled. Unable to keep his grip, he fell onto the ground, rolling over and over before stopping in a heap. The growl that left him as he sat up made the hair on the back of Katalina's neck stand on end. She scrambled farther into the back of the truck bed and banged on the glass window. "Go, Bass! Get me out of here!"

# CHAPTER 10

Ten minutes down the road, Katalina finally started to relax—until she saw a truck in the distance slowly gaining on them.

"Bass, we have company," she yelled.

"Shit! Hold on!"

Katalina barely had a chance to grasp the edge of the truck before Bass swerved off the road. The vehicle bumped violently over the rough terrain and into the woods. Bass weaved in and out of the trees at stupid speeds; branches collided with them, slashing at Katalina, huddled in the back. Arne stood on four spread legs, trying to keep upright; the look on his face indicated he wasn't impressed with the little detour. However, driving through the woods hadn't stopped Jackson from pursuing, and soon Katalina saw the battered blue truck following behind them.

"He's following!"

Katalina didn't hear Bass's answer. She screamed as she was thrown around when they turned sharply, bumping up onto another road. Arne's feet flew out from under him. He landed in a heap, skidding across the metal truck floor.

"I've got you, boy," Katalina said, wrapping her arms tightly around her dog.

"Nearly there!" Bass yelled. He swerved again, taking them into more woods.

"Nearly where?" They didn't seem to be anywhere, and she could hear tires screeching onto tarmac, so Jackson was still following.

Bass didn't answer; instead, he sped up, swerving through the maze of trees as if he knew the placement of every one. Katalina couldn't bear to look anymore. She was sure that at any minute they'd all be dead, with the truck wrapped around a tree trunk, but another few minutes of crazy driving and Bass came to an abrupt stop.

"Get in!"

Katalina jumped over the side, Arne following her, and they quickly climbed in. It wasn't until she shut the door and glanced behind her that she realized Jackson wasn't following them anymore.

"He gave up?" she asked, not quite believing it was true.

"We're on Dark Shadow land. I didn't think he'd risk an all-out w—" Bass's eyes widened. "Kat, what happened to you?" His hands gently touched her bleeding arm. "We need to get this out, Kat; otherwise, you'll heal with the glass still inside."

"Okay." She looked down at her arm for the first time, realizing it was lacerated and cut and that pieces of glass were embedded in her skin. The adrenaline from her escape began to fade when she took in her injuries.

Bass gently removed the glass from her shoulder and arm. Kat winced each time, biting her lip so she wouldn't cry out.

"There, all done. We'll stop at a gas station so you can freshen up, but I think it would be wise to leave before my father's enforcers arrive."

Katalina nodded, pulling her legs up to her chest and wrapping her arms around them. Bass glanced at her as he drove through the trees, slower this time.

"Tell me what happened, Katalina. Whose blood stains your skin?"

Katalina took a deep breath before speaking, "It's Toby's." She didn't miss the shocked look on his face, even if it was there for just a split second.

"Toby's, the young lad? I thought you liked him."

"I did . . . I do. Toby is the only friend I have there." She sucked in another breath. "I couldn't control it, Bass. Jackson had me locked up; he treated me like a prisoner and I was so angry. I . . . I lost it. I broke through the door and the wolf took over. I was so blinded by my rage I didn't even know it was Toby until I felt his bl . . . until . . ." She wiped at the tears running down her cheeks.

"Hey, Kat, it's okay. Losing control is perfectly normal after the first change, and your situation is very different. Jackson should have treated you better. He should have known. If anyone is to blame, it's him!"

"I don't ever want to change again," she whispered into her knees.

His hand ran through her hair. "So that's why you didn't change when you were running for the truck. I'm surprised you could control your wolf. No more worrying. You are safe now, Katalina."

Katalina turned her head to the side, her cheek resting on her knees. She looked at Bass with unshed tears in her eyes. "Am I? Am I ever going to be safe? Dark Shadow wants me dead and my own father wants to keep me as a prisoner. What was his plan? To just lock me up until he decides he wants me to have babies with Cage?"

Bass growled. His hand caressed her face. "I will never let anyone hurt you again. I'll keep you safe. Do you understand? You are mine, not his, and I will treat you like the queen you are. You'll never be locked up again."

*Mine* was such a possessive word, yet coming from Bass, it sounded anything but.

"Queen?"

"Yes, Katalina Winter, you are a queen, a very beautiful one," he said softly, brushing his thumb over her face. "Now, let's get you home."

"Do you think Jackson will come looking for me there?" she asked. "And your father, won't he wonder where you are?"

"I've taken care of my father, and as for Jackson, he'll most definitely come looking, but as long as you're with your family he can't just kidnap you. We may live outside of the law a lot of the time, but he couldn't get away with taking you in front of humans. I'll figure something out; just concentrate on dealing with all that's happened, and I'll worry about Jackson. Okay?"

"What do you mean, you've 'taken care of your father'?" she asked.

"Katalina, stop worrying," he answered, a little sharply.

Katalina nodded her response, wondering why he was being cagey.

He smiled at her warmly and Katalina chose to drop the subject. She trusted him. Sebastian Evernight made her feel whole. He was the missing piece she'd never realized she'd been searching for.

He'd rescued her. He was taking her home and he'd gone against his pack for her. He'd said she intrigued him. He'd also said she was beautiful, a queen; but what did all that really mean? She needed to understand what was between them; she needed a real answer.

"Why, Bass, why are you taking me home? Why are you helping me? And don't say I intrigue you. That's not an answer."

He glanced at her briefly, smiling. "You're mine."

"What does that even mean, Bass? Talk like a normal human being, will you?"

He chuckled softly at her.

"What's so funny?" she said, frustrated.

"You are. I'm not human, Kat. I'm a shifter, just like you, and I'm talking just like a shifter."

"Well, I was raised in the real world."

He looked at her, a sparkle in his eyes. "So you were, and in the *real world*, as you put it, I'd say, 'I love you, Katalina Winter.'"

Katalina couldn't speak, couldn't breathe. He loved her—this gorgeous, sexy boy loved her! How was that even possible? They'd had a handful of meetings and stolen kisses, yet her heart raced when his words registered.

"Your wolf was made for mine. They fit perfectly together. You are mine and I am yours. You're my mate, Katalina."

His words mesmerized her. He spoke with such certainty that she found herself squeaking out, "Mate?"

"Yes, Kat, mate." He chuckled again. "Can't you feel it?"

There was a rightness to his words. "I knew you were coming. Before I even saw the truck. I knew it was you. I didn't understand how, but deep down I knew."

He took her hand and brought it to his mouth, kissing each of her knuckles. "Because you are my mate."

Katalina moved closer to him, resting her head on his shoulder. She soaked up the heat of him. "I love you too, Bass." The words spilled from her without them even registering in her brain. She spoke from her heart. As soon as they filled the cab, she knew she had spoken the truth.

They drove on in silence, hands entwined, stopping only once to fill the truck with gas and to clean and bandage Katalina. Before long, Katalina dozed off, snuggled against Bass as he drove through the darkness. It had been a while since she'd felt truly safe, and with Bass she did. She trusted him.

She woke to Bass's fingers stroking her face, his soft voice whispering against her skin, "You're home, Katalina."

She sat up, feeling suddenly wide awake. It was still dark outside. A quick glance at the clock said it was one a.m.

"There's a car parked out front."

Katalina's eyes scanned the drive, finding the car. "It's my grandma's. She must be here." She leaped out of the truck, running for the front door, not caring about the sharp stones beneath her feet.

Bass was beside her in seconds, his dark eyes scanning all around. He positioned his body to protect. After a few loud bangs against the locked door, Katalina could hear feet shuffling toward the door. A light turned on above their heads, casting a dim light on them.

"Who is it?"

"It's me, Gram."

"Kat?" She heard the startled whisper and then the sound of a key turning.

*Crap, what am I going to say? Too late now.*

Just before the door opened, Katalina quickly kissed Bass on the mouth. "No mate talk in here. You'll freak Gram out."

Bass didn't get a chance to answer before the door swung wildly open, and Katalina was dragged into the arms of her grandma.

"Oh God, Kat, it's you. It's really you. I thought . . . Oh, thank God, you are safe. Let me get a look at you," Gram said, holding her at arm's length, her eyes focusing on the white dressings on her shoulder and down her arm.

"I'm all right, Gram, nothing serious."

"Well, I thought, after your mom and dad, well I . . ." her voice trailed off with emotion. Composing herself, she asked, "Where have you been, Kat?"

"Oh, I . . . um." *Shit, shit, shit!* She glanced at Bass out of the corner of her eye, hoping he had some idea of what to say.

"Her father found her on the side of the road, the other side of those woods. He took her to the hospital, but she couldn't remember who she was or what had happened when she woke."

Katalina's grandmother, just then noticing Bass, gave a startled squeak. "Kat, who is this?"

"Oh, um, he's my friend."

Bass took a step forward, offering his hand. "Sebastian Evernight, but my friends call me Bass. It's nice to meet you."

Grandma took his hand, still looking startled. "I'm Kat's grand-mother, M-Mary. You said her father?"

"Her biological father." Bass didn't seem fazed at all.

"And he didn't think it was important to inform her family she was alive?"

"I'm certain he wasn't aware she had any more family, and with Kat not having any memory, he was uncertain of what to do. Of course, when she recovered, I brought her straight here."

"Where is he?"

"Gram," Katalina jumped in, "I'm so tired. Can we talk about this in the morning, please?"

"Oh, yes, of course. You must be exhausted. Your friend can stay in the spare room."

They stepped over the threshold, Arne scampering in and curling up in his bed.

"It's so good to be home, hey, Arne?" Katalina smiled at her dog. "Come on, Bass. I'll show you the way."

With another quick hug, Katalina kissed her grandma on the cheek, took Bass's hand, and dragged him off down the hall.

Her home wasn't large. It had four bedrooms but the smallest was an office. Katalina walked past the spare room and realized her grandma had been asleep in there.

"He'll have to sleep in the office," said her grandma, who was trailing after them. "I . . . I couldn't bear to touch your parents' room."

Katalina swallowed down her tears as she walked past the next door. It was slightly ajar, and she caught a glimpse of her parents' bed, still unmade as if they would be jumping back into it any moment.

"Here it is," she said to Bass, overly cheerfully.

He pulled her in for a hug. "There is no need to put on a brave face for me, Kat."

"I'll be fine," she said, giving him a quick squeeze. "I'll go find some sheets. I'm afraid it's just a sofa bed. Hope that's okay?"

He answered with a soft kiss to her forehead. She returned a few minutes later with an armful of sheets and blankets. Bass took them from her before she could make his bed.

"I'm capable of making my own bed. You need to rest, Katalina. Is that your room?" he said with a nod toward the door opposite.

"Yep, bathroom is next door. Do you need anything else?"

Bass smiled, a wicked smile, glancing down the hall and then back at her. The silver flecks in his eyes sparkled as he spoke quietly. "Just one thing." His words wrapped around her, making her shiver. His lips touched hers, softly at first, teasing, and then with increased pressure, the kiss becoming urgent. She moaned into his mouth, opening up for his tongue to explore, to taste.

Katalina pulled away, breathless. "Bass, my grandma is just down the hall."

He smiled again, that naughty, wicked smile that made her weak in the knees. "She's asleep. Can't you hear her?"

"Of course I can't—" Katalina's words stuck in her throat. She *could* hear her. Her breaths were soft and even. "Wow."

"It's about time you started using your new senses, Katalina."

"I still need to sleep, Bass. I can't spend the rest of the night kissing you."

"Are you sure?" The hunger in his eyes made Katalina take a step back. If she didn't put some distance between them, she wouldn't be able to resist the pull she felt for him.

"Yes, stop that!" she said, trying to sound firm but failing. Part of her so desperately wanted to lose herself in him, but the more sensible part of her knew she needed to be well rested for the inevitable visit from Jackson.

"Stop what?"

"You know what. Stop looking at me like I'm edible!" She put her hands on her hips, trying not to smile.

He chuckled. "Okay, I'll behave." He dragged her back against his lean, hard body, kissing her softly. "Good night, Katalina Winter. I love you."

Katalina grinned stupidly. "I'll never tire of hearing that. Night."

Katalina closed her door, keeping her back to the room. She took a deep breath and prepared herself to turn around. It didn't matter how many deep breaths she took, the pain at seeing her room, the memories of her old life, a life she could never truly go back to, no matter how much she wanted it—the pain was too much. She let out a broken sob. Thick tears rolled down her face as she walked around her room, looking at pictures of her parents.

The door opened behind her. She knew it was Bass without looking; whenever he was near, she could feel the connection deep in her heart. "I'm fine, Bass," she said, wiping her face.

"No, you're not. I can feel your pain as if it's my own, Katalina."

She turned to face him, seeing for herself the pain he felt etched in his eyes. Being someone's mate was going to take some getting used to. It meant more than just loving someone. The connection was mind, body, and soul, as if the other person were your other half.

"You no longer need to suffer alone. Come here." Bass took her hand and led her to the bed.

"Wait, what are you doing?" she asked, startled. She'd never had a man in her room, never mind her bed.

"I'm going to hold you while you sleep." He got on the bed, dragging her with him and wrapping his arms around her.

"But my grandma, she'll freak out if she finds you in here." *I'm kinda freaking out, too.*

"Kat, I'll be out of here before she's even out of bed. Now sleep." He pulled the blanket around her, tangling his leg with hers. "Good night, my beautiful mate."

The urge to protest disappeared when he wrapped his arms around her. She didn't feel embarrassed or self-conscious. It simply felt right.

Katalina smiled into the darkness, entwining her fingers with Bass's. His heat seeped into her, his solid strength a soothing presence. The tears still came, but she wasn't alone. He never said a word, just held her impossibly tight, stroking his thumb in circles over her skin, leaving only when she cried herself out and fell into a deep, peaceful sleep.

# CHAPTER 11

Katalina woke to the sound of voices and the smell of bacon. She sat up, running her hands through her hair. It felt so surreal to be back in her bed. Pulling on a chunky cardigan, Katalina ventured out to the kitchen.

She stopped in her tracks as she rounded the corner. Bass was in the kitchen, cooking. She'd only ever seen him in his ragged jeans and the dark T-shirt he'd had on the previous night. Before her, Bass was wearing a baby-blue T-shirt, which clung to his lean, muscular body in all the right places. As he looked up, smiling, her breath caught. The color of his shirt brought out the faintest shade of blue in his impossibly dark eyes.

"Morning, Katalina," he said as she sat down next to her grandma.

"Hey," she answered, amazed she was able to keep the shake from her voice.

"Sebastian is cooking us breakfast," her grandma said, taking a bite of bacon.

"Yes, I can see that. I didn't know you could cook," she said to Bass.

"My father isn't the most gifted of cooks, so it was either learn or eat his rubbish. I learned."

Katalina laughed. Giving him another once-over, she sighed, content; he was sexy as sin and all hers.

"What about your mother?" Katalina's grandma asked.

"She died when I was a baby," he answered, placing a plate of bacon, eggs, and pancakes in front of Katalina.

"Oh, I'm sorry, dear."

"That's all right. I've had many years to come to terms with it."

Katalina searched for a change of subject. "What are you up so early for, Gram? You're never out of bed before ten."

Her grandma's face fell. "It's your mom and dad's funeral today, sweetie."

"Funeral? They haven't been buried yet?" The thought of them lying in some morgue made her feel queasy. She wrapped her arms tightly around her stomach, attempting to settle the emotions churning inside of her.

"No, darling, the police have only just finished their investigation, ruling it an accident."

"Oh." Katalina didn't feel much like eating anymore. She pushed her food around her plate, staring at it but focusing on nothing.

"What happened, Kat?" her grandmother asked her tentatively.

Katalina stared at the countertop a second longer. She didn't want to relive the horror from that night. *What do I even say? How am I supposed to explain everything without sounding insane?* She glanced up at Bass, wishing she'd asked him if there was some story she was supposed to be keeping to. After everything that had happened the previous day, she'd fallen asleep in the truck, and when she'd arrived, Katalina had been overwhelmed being back home. The last thing on her mind had been making up a story.

"It's all a bit of a blur. We were driving home from my birthday dinner and I saw a wolf running alongside the car. Dad turned to look and a group of wolves ran out onto the road. He didn't see them in time. The car skidded and flipped . . ."

"Wolves—the police said there were wolf prints all over the scene— but I couldn't believe wolves would be so close to town."

"Yes, Grandma, there were wolves," Katalina said sadly, glancing up to see how her grandma was reacting.

"But how did you get away, Kat? What happened after the crash?"

Kat's voice stuck in her throat. Images of that night tumbled through her mind: wolves tearing at her, pain everywhere, Arne saving her, and Toby carrying her away.

"A-Arne scared them off," she stuttered.

Her grandma frowned. "A German shepherd scared off a pack of wolves?"

"I—" There was a knock at the door.

"Oh, that must be your aunt." Her grandma got up and hurried off to answer the door.

Katalina pushed her plate away and put her head on the counter-top. "God, I can't do this. What am I supposed to say?"

He was at her side in a flash, murmuring, "Listen, Kat, you were in Henry Ford Hospital. Your father came that night to tell you about himself. He found you a few streets over, where you'd managed to run before collapsing. He never saw the crash. He didn't tell you who he was until your memory came back. Do you understand? That's the story."

"But I never went to the hospital, Bass. If they check—"

"There'll be records, Kat. I've pulled some strings."

"What . . . how?" Katalina glanced toward the front room; her grandma and aunt were coming. "Bass?" she whispered urgently.

"Do you trust me, Katalina?" he whispered.

"Yes."

"Then stick to that story," he whispered, kissing the top of her head as he stepped to the side of her.

"Kat!" her aunt shrieked, running toward her. "Oh, I'm so pleased you're okay."

"Hi, Aunt Susan," Katalina greeted, returning her hug, sadness lacing her words.

"And who is this, Kat?" she asked, looking Bass up and down.

"Susan, leave the boy alone," Katalina's grandma said.

"This is my friend, Bass. Is Dillon with you?"

"No, I left him at home with your uncle. A funeral is no place for a five-year-old."

Katalina nodded, taking a deep breath. She wasn't sure she was ready for a funeral either. As if sensing her feelings, Bass squeezed her shoulder. "Would you like to get some fresh air, Kat? I'm sure your aunt and grandmother have lots to do."

Katalina practically jumped off the stool and ran out the door. Every inch of the house reminded Katalina of some happy moment from her life and all she had lost. Just the thought of saying good-bye broke her heart. Being home, she could almost imagine nothing had changed, yet everything had. Even a second inside was too much; the air was thick, oppressive, to the point that breathing became too great an effort.

"Don't be long, Kat. You'll need to get ready," her grandmother called after Katalina's retreating figure.

The second Katalina was out of the house she leaned against the wall outside, her hands on her knees. The wind blew past her, making her shiver. The sky, gray and dreary, seemed fitting for the day.

She looked up as Bass approached. "I can't do this, Bass. I can't keep it together and lie about all that's happened. What was I thinking coming back here? I should have just disappeared."

"Katalina, that isn't true. You wouldn't have wanted your family to wonder what happened to you. I understand this isn't easy, but you've come back because you need to say good-bye." He cupped her cheeks and brought her head to his. "I'm here for you. You are going to get through this day and the day after that. I will always be here, to keep you going."

She nodded, wrapping her arms around him. "You look amazing in blue by the way." She grinned up at him, desperately wanting to think of something other than her parents' funeral.

"Your aunt seemed to think so, too."

Katalina burst out laughing, amazed that, even with a heavy heart, he was able to make her smile. "Come on. I'll show you around the impressive garden," she said sarcastically with a wave of her hand.

The garden wasn't a bad size but consisted of mostly lawn and a few shrubs. It took them all of two minutes to walk the garden, and in that time, more people had arrived at the house: friends and distant relatives she hardly knew, all of them wanting to know her story. Katalina gave them vague answers, sticking to the things Bass had told her, while never letting go of his hand. He was her anchor, the only thing keeping her grounded and out of the darkness of her grief.

"Come on," Katalina whispered to him, weaving through the mass of bodies. Bass in tow, she escaped to her room. "Close the door."

"As you wish," he said with a bow.

"Funny!" she muttered, opening her wardrobe. "I think I have one plain, boring black dress in here somewhere."

"Kat, I'm not exactly dressed in funeral attire," Bass observed, looking down at himself.

Kat tossed a dress on her bed. Turning, she looked at him. "Have you got any black jeans?"

"Yes, but black jeans aren't appropriate either."

"So what? No one will notice. They'll be too distracted by your face."

He chuckled at her. "I'll take that as a compliment."

"Oh yes, you definitely should." She walked toward him, planting a kiss on his mouth. "Now, go find your jeans while I get dressed."

By the time he returned, Katalina had dressed in her knee-length dress. It hugged her waist before flaring out. She'd paired it with black tights and black boots with a small heel.

"How you doing, Kat? I'm certain you weren't expecting to come home to this."

"Not really. Part of me is pleased I'm here for it, the other just wishes I had a grave to visit already. It's just so hard dealing with all those people, asking me questions I can't answer."

"You'll get through this. I'll be right beside you, every step of the way."

Katalina rested her head on his shoulder and took his hand. "Thanks," she whispered softly. "Well, I suppose we best go back out there."

She reached for the door but Bass called her back. "Kat, have you seen this?"

Turning, Katalina looked in the direction he pointed and saw a black box, tied with a red bow.

"Oh, it must be a birthday present." She gulped loudly, slowly making her way to the box, not quite sure she wanted to see its contents. She knew it was from her parents as she tentatively picked up the gift.

She read the label aloud.

*An extra one for my precious girl. I can't believe you are eighteen already! Happy Birthday, my winter girl! Love, Mom xoxo P.S. I know, I go crazy with the white!*

Katalina smiled as tears filled her eyes.

"What does she mean *crazy with the white?*" Bass asked from behind her.

Katalina laughed sadly. "Mom had an obsession with buying me all things white; she called me her winter girl. I'm not sure I have the strength to open this."

"I think you'll be surprised at the strength you possess, Katalina Winter," he murmured against her ear.

She took a deep breath, her chest rising high, and pulled the bow. The red ribbon tumbled to the floor, followed by the lid. Katalina pulled the white fur coat from the box. Her knees gave out, and she dropped to the floor with a sob, clutching the coat to her chest.

"Oh, Mom," she sobbed.

"Baby," Bass soothed, wrapping himself around her. "It's as white as your wolf fur. I do hope it's not real, though."

Katalina laughed through her tears. "Maybe it's wolf."

She ran her hands over the coat, picturing her mother doing the same when she bought it from the store.

"You should wear it today," Bass suggested.

"It's the wrong color for a funeral."

"I think your mom would have loved for you to wear her gift. Get up. Come and try it on." He held her hand and pulled her to her feet. "My beautiful winter wolf," he murmured in her ear, making her smile.

There was a knock at the door. "Kat, it's time to go," her grandma called through the door.

Katalina huffed out a breath. Glancing at herself in the mirror one last time, she nodded at her pale reflection. *You can do this, Kat. Just keep it together for the next few hours.*

"Coming, Gram."

# CHAPTER 12

The funeral passed in a blur. Katalina couldn't seem to focus on any-thing but the grief churning inside of her. She was the focus of warm condolences and reassuring pats on her arm, but none of it mattered. Her parents were gone. They were dead. She'd never see them again. All that kept her upright was the firm grip of Bass's hand, his strong, steady presence.

"Kat? Katalina?"

Katalina focused on her grandma's face.

"Kat, the police, they're here to see you," her grandma said gently, nodding toward the unmarked car parked at the edge of the graveyard. Detectives leaned against it.

"Police, now?" she asked, bewildered.

"I'm sorry, Kat. Susan tried to get rid of them but they won't leave. Just answer their questions and then it'll be over with."

"Okay," she whispered, taking an uneasy step toward them.

"I think it would be best if you stayed here, Sebastian," her grand-mother added.

Bass looked a little put out but stayed behind.

Katalina walked slowly toward the two men, feeling lost now that Bass wasn't by her side. She weaved between the headstones, trailing after her grandmother and glancing back at Bass every now and then. When she reached the detectives, she took one final look at him and then took a deep breath, preparing herself for the questions.

"Miss Winter?"

Katalina focused on the men and nodded.

"We're very sorry to interrupt, today of all days, but we're hoping you can shed some light on a few things," the oldest of the detectives said.

Katalina nodded again. She stuck her hands in her pockets to hide the fact they were trembling.

"Well, why don't you start off by telling us what happened the night of the crash?'

Katalina opened her mouth to speak but couldn't voice the horrors of the night. It was all too much, too devastating. She didn't want to recall the night again.

"There were wolves, weren't there, Kat?" her grandmother prompted with a reassuring pat.

"Yes . . . they followed the car. Dad took his eyes off the road for a second and"—she sucked in a breath—"then they ran out in front of the car. It flipped." Katalina closed her eyes, forcing the images, the memories away.

"But you made it out of the car?" the detective asked.

"Yes," she answered in a small voice.

"But how did you get away?"

"My dog came."

"Your dog saved you from a pack of wolves?" he asked, disbelief evident on his face.

Katalina looked the detective in the eye. "Yes," she said sternly.

"So, then your biological father finds you a few streets over, and rushes you to the hospital. This is what your grandmother tells us."

Katalina nodded.

"Why not inform the rest of your family you were safe?"

"She had no memories! I've told you this already," Katalina's grandmother snapped.

"We'd just like to hear Miss Winter's version of events."

"I came home as soon as I had my memory back. Now, if that's all, I'm at my parents' funeral." Katalina didn't wait to see if the detectives had any more questions. She turned on her heels, marching back to Bass.

"Are you all right?" he asked as she approached.

Katalina didn't dare speak for fear of crying, so she nodded instead.

Her grandmother returned a few minutes later, having sent the police on their way. "Kat, we must get going. We'll be late for the wake."

*Wake . . . more people, more questions.*

"Kat?"

Katalina opened her mouth to speak but couldn't find the words. Fresh tears pooled in her eyes. She blinked rapidly, trying to force them back.

Bass stepped in. "I think Katalina has had enough for one day. I'll walk her home. I think she needs a little time alone."

"Oh, right, yes—it's been a hard morning. We'll see you at home, Kat," her grandma said.

Katalina hugged her grandmother, and then followed Bass as he guided her along. She was lost in her dark thoughts, replaying the crash over and over, looking for some way to have saved her parents. Her feet squelched in the slushy snow, and the wind bit at her face, raw from tears. Her whole body felt like ice, right down to her broken, torn soul. Her only source of warmth came from Bass's hand, still strong in hers.

"Where are we going?" she asked, after realizing they'd been walking into the woods for the last few minutes.

"We are going to have a run. It will make you feel better," he explained, stopping.

"A run?"

"Yes," he smiled, pulling his coat and T-shirt off.

"A naked run?" she smirked.

"Don't be a smart-ass, Kat." He slipped his jeans off and then his boxers.

Katalina gave a startled squeak, spinning around so he was at her back. "Bass, I don't want to change again, and I'm not sure running around as wolves is the best idea."

"I'll keep you safe. Now, come on, Kat, undress. I've seen it all before," he said, his tone flirty.

"Bass!"

He answered by pressing a cold wolf nose against her leg.

"Fine!" she snapped, carefully putting her coat on top of his clothes so it wouldn't get dirty. The rest of her clothes followed. *Right, Kat, easy peasy. You're a shifter; changing should be a piece of cake.*

Bass barked at her.

"Okay, okay, grumpy wolf!"

She closed her eyes, cleared her mind, and pictured her wolf. The pain this time wasn't so bad. She bit her lip as she collapsed onto her knees, and seconds later, she took a step forward on wolf paws.

Bass had been right. She felt instantly better. It wasn't that the pain and grief she felt had gone; rather, it dulled. It was as if the wolf couldn't process her feelings, making them easier to deal with. Bass took off at a steady run. Following him, Katalina marveled at the simple pleasure of feeling the wind weave through her fur, and the feel of dirt between her paws. They couldn't run very far; the woodland wasn't large and they easily covered the length of it in minutes, but it was enough. Twenty minutes of leisurely running back and forth between the trees helped Katalina cope with her emotions.

"Feel better?" Bass asked as he slung his coat on.

Katalina turned, now fully dressed, to face him. "Yes, but I'm ready to go home now."

"As you wish, my queen," he replied with a devilish smile and a bow.

"Stop with the queen, Bass," she said, hitting him playfully on the arm.

Bass stopped suddenly, dragging her into his arms. He dipped her low, whispering, "Why? You are the ruler of my heart, Katalina Winter. There is nothing I wouldn't do for you. No line I wouldn't cross. You are mine. The soul mate for both my halves." He kissed her hard and fast.

Katalina shook her head, clearing the desire fogging her mind. "Sometimes I wonder if you're even real. People don't talk like that in the real world."

"Why do you want to live in this *real world* then, Kat? Come with me into the world of wolves and soul mates." He spoke in a joking tone, but she could tell by the look in his eyes he was deadly serious, and it scared her. She wasn't afraid that he may lead her into another life; rather, she was worried that she'd want this new life too much and forget she'd once lived as if human.

Katalina searched for something meaningful to say. *I love you* just didn't seem to do Bass justice, but before she could open her mouth, she found herself twisted around as Bass spun her behind him with a savage growl.

"Bass?" Katalina gasped.

"Someone is stalking us. Stay behind me, Katalina."

Katalina scanned the trees, her heart kicking up a gear when she imagined Jackson and the enforcers racing from the trees and taking her away. But it wasn't Jackson who appeared. It was Cage, his hands held up in a submissive gesture.

"I just want to talk," he said in a soft voice.

"How can I trust you?" Katalina asked, placing her hand on Bass's shoulder, hoping to calm him.

Cage actually looked hurt. "I guess I deserve that. The last few days I haven't been very kind to you."

Katalina didn't confirm it. There was no need.

"But please, Kat, I've come to warn you and to apologize. Can we talk? Alone?"

"She's not going anywhere with you!" Bass growled, still not moving from his defensive stance.

"Please," Cage begged.

"Talk, Cage. Whatever you've come to say can be said in front of Bass."

Cage took a step forward, a small smile of relief on his lips. "Okay."

"Stay where you are!" Bass ground out.

"Bass, he's hardly going to attack me in broad daylight, with you beside me. I'm sure he can come closer."

"As you wish." Bass took a small step, putting himself beside Katalina, but his eyes never left Cage.

"I'm sorry, Kat, okay? I've really messed up. All I ever wanted was to protect you, and I went along with Jackson—not because I thought he was right, but because I didn't want to go against my alpha. I see now that was a big mistake."

"I thought you were my friend, Cage, but you treated me as a prisoner, just like him."

"I know and I'm sorry. I came to make it up to you, to warn you. I've gone against your father's wishes to do this, Kat. Even now my wolf is pacing."

"Warn me about what?" she asked, feeling on edge.

"Jackson . . . he's . . . he's sent his enforcers to bring you back, three of them. They're to snatch you when you're alone." He spoke the sentence in one big rush as if it pained him to tell her.

"And you? You're his enforcer, too."

"I won't do it, Kat. You have the right to mourn your parents in peace. You'll come home when you're ready."

"This is my home, Cage."

He didn't respond, but she saw the hurt in his eyes.

"Three enforcers? Their orders are to take her when she's alone?" Bass asked.

"That was the order, but Jackson is bound to find out I've warned you. He may get desperate. Maybe I should stay, Kat, to protect you."

A growl cut off Katalina's reply. "I can handle three. Katalina has no need for you."

Cage growled back, his eyes filling with anger.

"Hey! No fighting!" Katalina yelled before they had a chance to start. Looking at the two of them, she became acutely aware they were more than just men.

"Is this what you want, Kat? You want me to leave?" Cage asked.

Katalina sighed, the heavy feeling of dread settling in her stomach. "It was hard enough explaining Bass. I can't have you hanging around, too, Cage. You should go home to your family, to Toby."

He nodded, turning away. He headed for the trees, but before he reached them, he paused. Half turning, he asked quietly, "Does he make you happy?"

"Yes," she answered honestly.

"It was supposed to be me," he said, so quietly she was sure she only heard him because of her new wolf abilities.

Katalina walked toward him; she couldn't help it. She felt terrible for making him so sad. She could almost feel the sorrow seeping off him.

"Kat," Bass warned.

"He won't hurt me, Bass. Trust me."

Katalina walked over to Cage, who still stood on the edge of the forest, his back to her, shoulders slumped.

"Cage," she whispered, touching his arm.

It broke her when he looked at her, tears in his eyes. "I love you, Kat. I've been waiting my whole life for you, and now I've messed everything up."

She pulled in a deep breath, thinking of the right words to say. "Cage, you don't love me, not really. You love the idea of me. You love the life everyone has told you that you should live. I'm not the girl they told you about. I never have been. Maybe it's time to stop doing as you are asked, and really think about what you want. One day you're going to meet the girl you're supposed to be with, your mate, and you'll understand what I mean. I'm sorry, Cage—truly I am—but I love Bass."

A tear escaped, trailing slowly over his cheek. Katalina reached up on her toes and kissed the tear away. "Good-bye, Cage," she whispered.

When she looked back minutes later, he remained standing where she'd left him.

"Stop beating yourself up, Katalina. It is not your fault you do not feel the same."

"I didn't want to hurt him, Bass. He saved me, both him and Toby. I would be dead right now if they hadn't come."

"He'll get over it," Bass muttered.

"Would you?" Katalina snapped.

"No . . . but we are different. We are mates. Your wolf doesn't want him; she wants me. It would have never worked, and if your father were thinking straight, he'd know he could never push two shifters together. Our wolves choose; it has always been that way."

"I don't think Jackson has thought straight since Winter died."

# CHAPTER 13

They'd been walking for a while when Katalina finally saw her home ahead. She didn't feel the cold like she used to, but her face still stung from the constant bite of freezing wind against her skin. A surge of joy filled her as she saw her house. Her feet quickened their pace, excitement flowing through her blood until reality hit her and her stomach dropped. It was her house, her home, but the reason behind her happiness had been ripped away from her forever. For a second, she'd forgotten her parents were dead. For one glorious second, she'd managed to forget that she'd just watched their coffins being lowered into the earth.

Her knees buckled as she noticed the charred ground. Immediately, memories of the attack overwhelmed her: images, sounds, the fear. It was as if she was there again, reliving the horror, watching her parents burn as wolves sunk their teeth into her flesh, dragging her away from her family as if she were nothing but game. She heard distant barking; she felt a sudden feeling of hope that Arne might save her, and then she remembered the pack of wolves trying to devour her.

"No, Arne!"

She didn't want her dog to die, too. She couldn't lose them all.

It was too late. He was there, licking her face, whining . . .

"Katalina, baby, come back to me," the voice whispered around her.

*Wait . . . that voice doesn't belong to this nightmare.*

"Katalina Winter, look at me! You are here. You are safe!" The edge of a growl, the strength of a command.

Her eyes focused through the blur of tears and found his dark eyes.

"Katalina." His words were harsh, commanding, but his eyes and his touch held so much love that the horrifying images cleared.

She took his hand and let him pull her up. "Hey, boy," she croaked, ruffling the fur on Arne's head with her hand.

"Are you all right?" Bass asked softly.

"For now."

"Come on. Let's get you inside."

They walked in silence to the house; no one had returned yet, much to Katalina's relief. She needed some peace, some time to work through her emotions. She curled up into the corner of the sofa with Arne at her feet, his head resting on her legs.

"Something to drink?" Bass asked.

She looked up and nodded. "Tea please."

What felt like seconds later, Bass returned with two mugs, one filled with steaming tea for her. She caught the whiff of coffee from his mug and pulled a face.

"What? Do you not like coffee?" Bass laughed.

"I hate the smell."

He circled his mug under his nose, sighing as he breathed deeply. "Nonsense, it's wonderful."

She leaned her head on his shoulder. "If you say so."

They drank in silence for a while, enjoying the quiet, simple moment together, without any distractions.

"Tell me about them," Bass said quietly, squeezing her hand.

Katalina stood up and collected an album from the shelf. She turned to the first page. "They adopted me a few months before I turned one. My mother said I was so quiet when they first brought me home. I never spoke or cried. She said I used to sit on the floor and just watch the world go by, but never interacted."

She flipped the pages. "This is my first birthday. Mom went all out on parties. She said I'd been with them for six months before I actually started to talk beyond asking for things. Maybe I was traumatized from watching Winter die? I don't remember."

"What's the first thing you remember?" Bass asked.

A smile lit her face. "Mom brought this cat home, just before I turned three." She flipped a few pages. "Look, there it is."

"It doesn't look very happy," Bass laughed, his finger tracing over the little girl hugging a tabby cat.

"It hated me, but I never let it escape. It would hiss and screech at me. Mom told me it ran away, but I'm certain she found it a new home."

"You realize why it hated you?"

Katalina frowned. "Oh! I'm a wolf. It would have been able to sense that?"

"Yes."

"When did you get Arne?"

"On my tenth birthday." She turned a few more pages. "He was the cutest puppy ever—weren't you, boy?" She kissed Arne's head when he looked up at her.

"Hey! Where's mine?"

Katalina laughed as Bass dragged her onto his lap. She found his lips easily. Running her hands up his shoulders and tangling them into his hair, Katalina forgot the photo album as she and Bass got lost in the feel of one another. The love and desire she felt for Bass pushed back Katalina's grief. Her hands roamed his body. Slipping her hands under his T-shirt, her nails grazed over his smooth skin.

He moaned into her mouth, his hands gripping her waist tighter, fingers digging into flesh. He lifted her and laid her onto the sofa, trapping her body with his.

"Bass," she gasped.

He smiled cheekily, crushing his mouth to hers.

She wasn't sure how long she lay trapped beneath him, her body on fire, every part of her craving his touch, before he suddenly pulled away, jumping onto the sofa chair.

"Bass?" she asked breathlessly, lifting up on her elbows. "What's wrong?"

He nodded toward the door. "Company."

At first, she couldn't hear anything, but then she really concentrated and heard tires driving over gravel.

"How do you do that? I have to really concentrate to hear them."

He smiled. "You've been a full shifter for only a few days, Kat. Give it time, and before you know it, every sense you have will be heightened. Katalina, I think you'd best straighten your dress and hair," he said with a wink.

"What? Oh . . ." She looked down at her dress; the hem had ridden up to the top of her thighs.

Katalina jumped to her feet, straightened her hair in the mirror, and wiggled her dress back down. "You don't look much better yourself," she laughed, patting his hair down. By the time her grandmother and aunt walked in, she'd slumped back onto the sofa and found something to watch on TV.

"Hi," she called as they walked into the kitchen, carrying boxes of food. "Need help?"

"There's a few more in the car," Aunt Susan replied.

Katalina stood, but Bass stopped her. "I'll get them."

"Bass, I'm not an invalid."

He kissed her cheek. "I know that. I would rather you stayed inside, where it's safe and no one can take you away from me."

"Go on then," she huffed, walking into the kitchen. "Bass is fetching the rest," she said, sitting next to her aunt at the breakfast bar.

"Here, try this," her aunt instructed, sliding a box toward her. "You won't believe this chocolate cake!" Her aunt smiled.

Her grandmother passed her a spoon.

"Wow, looks amazing," Katalina said, lifting the lid of the box.

Katalina had already shoveled three spoonfuls into her mouth when Bass came in carrying an armful of boxes. "Where would you like these?" he asked.

"Just there is fine," Katalina's grandmother replied. "I hope you two are hungry. There is enough food left to feed a village."

"Bass! Try this. It's so good." Katalina smiled, holding a spoonful of cake out to him.

He smiled warmly at her, closing his mouth around the spoon. "Mmm," he moaned, bending and kissing her softly. "Perfect," he murmured, looking into her eyes.

They pulled apart, realizing what they'd done. Katalina looked at Bass, wide-eyed. The expression on his face confirmed he'd never been so caught up in someone that he forgot the situation he was in.

Her grandmother cleared her throat loudly. "Come help me with something, will you, Sebastian?"

Bass dragged his eyes from Katalina's. "Yes . . . of course," he answered, looking a little ruffled.

Katalina stuffed another mouthful of cake into her mouth, hoping her aunt wouldn't say anything.

"Enough cake, Kat. Come walk with me." She didn't have much choice; her aunt hooked her arm through Katalina's and led her outside.

Katalina kept silent as she walked around the garden, dreading what her aunt would say.

"Kat, you're eighteen now, an adult, free to do as you wish. I'm not sure what your mom would have said about Bass. This should have been a conversation you had with your mother, but nothing has gone as it should, has it?"

"No," Katalina agreed.

"I can see the attraction, Kat. He's one fine-looking young man."

"Aunt Susan," Katalina groaned in embarrassment.

"What? I'm not that old, Kat. I'm worried about you, though. Your grandma has filled me in on what she knows, and a lot has happened to you over the past couple of weeks. Do you not think it's a bit soon to be meeting someone?"

"It's not like I'm planning on marrying him," Katalina muttered, feeling guilty for lying. He was her soul mate. She couldn't imagine life without him, but how would she explain that to her aunt?

"But it's not a fleeting relationship, is it? What just happened in there . . . a simple kiss, but you were both lost in your own world. Yes, I understand how everything is exciting when you first meet, but from what I've seen, it's pretty serious."

"No, it's not just fleeting, but I'm not stupid, Susan. I can take care of myself and I'm old enough to decide who I see," Katalina replied, irritated. She'd always been sensible, stayed out of trouble. She deserved a little credit for that.

"Just be careful, okay? You've just lost your parents. Maybe you should mourn them before you go falling in love?"

Katalina turned sharply. She stood in front of her aunt in anger. Her wolf pushed against her skin as her emotions rose to the surface. Hands clenched into fists, she ground out, "Is that what you think? That I'm so caught up in my love for Bass that I've not even realized my mom and dad are dead? Well, let me tell you something, *Susan*. I saw them die! I saw the car burst into flames while wolves were attacking me. I will never ever forget that. The image will be etched in my mind for eternity. Some days, it feels like I might drown in the sadness closing around me. Bass has been the only one keeping me going. So much has happened and he's been there every step of the way."

She turned on her heel and stormed off. Her aunt called her back, but she'd reached her limit and needed to be alone. It was as though her wolf was pacing inside of her mind, snapping and snarling; angry, so angry. Katalina paced the garden, taking deep breaths. She couldn't lose control again. Toby was a shifter; he healed quickly. Her aunt and grandma, though, were only human.

She realized her mistake too late. She was alone. Susan had long since gone back into the house, and Katalina had ventured to the far end of the garden, which backed up to a small stand of trees and brushland. There were houses on either side, but she was vulnerable where she was at that moment. Her wolf paced for a whole different reason; her hackles rose. Katalina felt the urge to change. As a wolf, she could protect herself better. But she lived on the outskirts of town, a town where people were unaccustomed to seeing wolves wandering around. If her aunt or grandmother saw her, how would she explain the fact that she was a shifter?

Katalina backed away, slowly and carefully moving over the ground, never taking her eyes off the fence line. She'd managed only a few steps when someone appeared at the fence. She didn't recognize him, but then, she'd only met one other enforcer apart from Cage. His chest was bare and she guessed the rest of him was too, but the shrub around the fence hid his lower body from view. She heard movement and saw the outlines of two wolves standing on either side of him.

"Katalina, we won't hurt you. We've just come to take you home. You're not safe here."

She took another step back. "This is my home."

"Kat—can I call you Kat? Please don't make this any harder than it is." He held his hands up, palms out.

"It's not hard at all. Just leave. Tell Jackson I'll never be forced into being in his pack."

His hands dropped. Katalina took another step back, her heart racing so fast she could hardly hear his reply over the pulsing blood running through her head. "I'm afraid I can't do that, Katalina. I have orders and I don't disobey my alpha."

Katalina turned and ran. She heard the rattle of the fence. The garden wasn't long, but the enforcer was fast and his hand latched onto her arm before she could make it to the house. Katalina gasped from his harsh grip. Twisting her body around, she slapped him across the face as she pulled with all her strength, trying to escape.

"Bitch," he muttered, yanking at her. She lost her footing.

A growl escaped her as she pushed against him. "Get off me!" Her knee came up, slamming between his legs. He fell back with a grunt, finally letting go of Katalina's arm. A savage growl came from behind the fence, but the enforcer held his hand up, signaling for the wolf to hold position.

"Hold. I can handle the bitch," the enforcer growled, looking feral.

Fear left Katalina. Instead of running, she stood her ground, feeling the strength of her wolf close to the surface.

Before the enforcer could take a step toward her, Bass appeared beside her, his body angled slightly in front of her.

"I leave you alone for five minutes and you find some stray mutts for me to play with." Bass's voice was oddly calm and yet held the savage, untamed note of his wolf.

"They were just leaving, weren't you? Sorry, I never caught your name," Katalina replied with venom.

"We're not leaving without you," the enforcer demanded.

"She's going nowhere with you," Bass growled.

The enforcer let out a bitter laugh. "Are you going to stop us? You do realize there are three of us and one of you."

Bass simply smiled.

"Katalina?" Her grandmother's voice came from inside the house.

The enforcer's eyes darted toward the house and back.

"Do you really want to explain to your alpha how you exposed yourself to humans? I'm sure Katalina's grandmother will have cops around the house when she realizes some savages want to take her granddaughter away. I'm happy to fight, of course, if you feel the need."

"This isn't over!" the intruder spat, before turning on his heel and disappearing over the fence.

"There you are," her grandmother hollered into the garden. "I've been calling you. I've set out some leftovers for supper. Come inside."

Katalina took a deep breath and slipped her hand into Bass's. "Coming," she called back, overly cheerful.

"Are you all right?" Bass whispered as they walked toward the back door.

"Never better."

# CHAPTER 14

Later that day when the sun had set and everyone had gone to bed, Katalina lay awake, her mind going over the day. She shot upright in bed when the sound of her door opening disturbed her. She closed her hand around the baseball bat hidden under the covers.

"Ugh, Bass, you scared me," she sighed, when his smiling face appeared.

"Katalina, if you'd have used your senses, you would have known it was me." His eyes settled on the bat she still held. "Planning on knocking me out?" he joked.

"Oh . . . no, of course not, but I'm not exactly feeling too safe right now."

"Katalina," he whispered, coming to her side, "you are safe. I promise. I'll never let anyone hurt you."

"They could have taken me today, Bass," she answered, sounding rattled.

"There was never a chance of that happening. I sensed them approach. I just couldn't get away from your grandmother, but you handled yourself beautifully, Kat. You're stronger than you think."

"If you say so," she muttered.

"I know so," he replied, leaning in for a kiss.

Pulling back from his kiss, she asked, "What are you doing here anyway? You'll be kicked out of the house if you're found."

"Everyone's asleep. Although, I think your aunt forced herself to stay awake for a while, thinking I'd be sneaking in."

"Which you are," Katalina smiled, feeling less afraid now that he was with her.

He smiled cheekily. "I've come to steal you away."

"What?" She frowned.

"Come run with me."

"Running? It's the middle of the night," Katalina said, sounding skeptical.

"I know. The best time to not be seen."

"You mean you want to go out and run around as wolves? What about Jackson's men?"

"I'll deal with them."

"I don't know, Bass. I'd rather just try to sleep."

"Okay." He kissed her lips. "I'll be back in a bit."

"You're still going?"

"Yes, Kat. I'm not used to staying human for such a long period. If I do not allow my wolf freedom, he will become unsettled."

"Oh . . . okay, be careful."

He kissed her hungrily, cupping her face. "I will," he breathed into her mouth, making her shudder.

He slipped out the window. Katalina lay on her side staring out the window, imagining Bass changing into his black wolf, blending into the night as if he were a part of it. Part of her longed to join him, but she pushed that part away, not wanting to acknowledge that her wolf was becoming as much a part of her as her human side. With a sigh, she turned over, roughly wrapping the covers around her shoulders, and forced her eyes to stay shut.

She tossed and turned for a long time, feeling at war with herself, wanting to join Bass and worrying if he was safe. She wanted to sleep and pretend she was still the normal girl she'd been before she'd turned eighteen. Her last glance at the clock showed it to be two thirty a.m. Bass had been gone for over an hour. She imagined the three enforcers tracking him down and attacking him. She almost climbed out of bed and went into the night looking for him.

"Stop it, Kat! Bass isn't stupid. He'll be fine. Now, go to sleep," she muttered to herself, flopping back onto the mattress, punching the pillow as if it was at fault for her inability to fall asleep.

\*\*\*\*\*

Hands touched her. Her bed dipped from the weight of another . . .

Katalina reacted on instinct. Her wolf surged within her, forcing her into action. Her elbow connected with flesh as her hand gripped the intruder's neck. The savage snarl that echoed around the room startled even Katalina.

Her eyes focused on the person she was pinning to the bed. "Bass?" Her eyes widened, her hand jumping back. "Oh, God, Bass, are you all right?" She jumped away from him, frightened her body might act on its own accord again. "I'm so sorry. I just . . . I'm not sure. I just acted, I guess."

Bass sat up, rubbing his neck, and laughed low. "Well, that will teach me to climb into your bed uninvited."

Katalina covered her face with her hands. "Bass, this is not funny. I just attacked you," she mumbled through her fingers.

"It's a little funny."

Katalina flopped back with a sigh. "What were you doing, anyway?"

"Going to sleep."

"What made you think you could just climb in bed with me?"

"Well, you are my mate. I've been out running for most the night. I just wanted to curl up next to you and sleep."

Katalina wanted to be mad at him, but her heart melted at his words. She loved to see the soft, loving side of him, the part that needed her more than anything else. To the outside world, he was formal, polite. Only Katalina saw his funny, caring side.

She pulled the covers back. "Come on then."

He was about to climb back under the covers when his head angled to the door. She heard it the second after he did: someone was walking toward her room. Their eyes met and then Bass was gone. Katalina pulled the covers up to her chin, closing her eyes just as her door opened. She kept still, listening for the moment her aunt left.

"Kat?" Susan whispered from the doorway. She stood there a moment longer before closing the door again and returning to bed.

When the house fell silent, Katalina let out her breath and rolled over. Half sitting up, she scanned her room for Bass; at first glance she couldn't see him, but then, when she really looked, using her wolf senses, she could see him in the far corner of her room, hidden in shadows. He would be invisible to the human eye.

"Sometimes I think you become a shadow yourself," she whispered as he stepped into the moonlight.

A smile lit his face, all charm with just the slightest touch of wickedness. "Now, where were we?"

She pulled the covers back again. "I think I was inviting you into my bed." She looked up at him through long lashes, feeling suddenly shy.

His eyes softened, the wicked edge of his smile changing to warmth and love. His arms wrapped around her, pulling her flush against his body. "Good night, my beautiful Katalina," he murmured against her bare shoulder, placing a soft kiss over her tingling skin.

Katalina closed her eyes and relaxed into his hold. The tension she felt melted away as his smell, his warmth, and his love surrounded her. In his arms, nothing could touch her and everything was right in the world.

# CHAPTER 15

When Katalina woke, she lay for a few blissful seconds, allowing happiness to trickle through her. She smiled at Bass's sleeping face so close to hers, at his legs tangled around her, his arms holding her so gently. In those few seconds her life was perfect, but then the memories returned. She'd buried her parents yesterday. She'd been threatened by Jackson's enforcers.

Trying to calm the growing tension within her, she sucked in a deep breath and focused on Bass's face. He looked so peaceful in sleep; he looked his age. She constantly had to remind herself he was only a year older than she was. The way he talked and the views he had on the world were more typical of an older person. She wondered if it was merely because he was a shifter, or maybe because of the way he'd been brought up.

He stirred in his sleep, a slight frown marring his perfect forehead. Katalina glanced at the clock; it was six a.m. Bass had been asleep for only a few hours. She didn't want to wake him yet. Gently slipping out of his hold, she threw on her robe and crept out of the room.

The house was silent, but as she walked into the living room, she saw she wasn't the only person awake.

"Hey," she said to her aunt, as she headed to the kitchen. "Tea?"

"Nope, still full." She lifted her mug, not taking her eyes off the paperwork scattered around her.

Katalina made her cup of tea and then sat opposite her aunt.

"When are you heading home? Dillon must be missing you."

Her aunt paused and smiled but still didn't look at Katalina. "Yes, he does. Today I hope, if I can sort through all of this first."

Katalina took a sip of her tea and then looked at the papers all over the table: bills, letters, words she didn't understand.

"What is all this?"

"Nothing for you to worry about, Kat."

"Aunt Susan?"

Her aunt sighed and put down the papers in her hands. "I'm afraid your parents weren't very prepared."

"What do you mean?"

"The life insurance they had doesn't cover the mortgage. I suppose they didn't plan on leaving so early. They have a small sum of savings that was for your college fund, but that's it, Kat. Looking at all this, I can't find any way out of selling the house."

"What?" Katalina choked on the word. "But this is my home."

"I know, Kat, but there is no other way. You'll have to come live with me, or your grandma."

Tears fill Katalina's eyes. She gulped back the lump in her throat. "But all my memories are here. I've lost Mom and Dad. I can't lose my memories, too."

"Oh, sweetie"—her aunt stood and came around to Katalina, taking her in her arms—"no one can ever take your memories away. Memories are how we live on. Your parents will never truly be gone because they'll live on in you. In the way you act, the things you do, they'll have influenced you. Your memories are locked up here, Kat"—she pointed a finger to her head—"forever in your mind. It doesn't matter where you live."

Katalina nodded, scared to talk in case opening her mouth would set loose the tidal wave of tears inside of her.

"You two girls are up early," her grandma said as she walked past them.

Susan pulled away from Katalina and sat back in her seat. "Trying to get the rest of this paperwork sorted for you before I leave this afternoon."

"And you, Kat?" her grandma asked.

Katalina took a deep breath before answering, "Couldn't sleep."

"Well, might as well wake up Sebastian. We can all have breakfast together." Grandma started to walk out of the kitchen.

Katalina jumped from her chair, knocking it to the floor. "I'll get him, Gram," she called, running after her.

"Don't be silly, dear. I'll knock first."

Katalina's heart hammered in her chest and she felt slightly woozy, her mind searched for some explanation as to why he wasn't in his bed, but hers. She came up empty; all she could do was stand by looking stupid, waiting for the arguments to come.

Her grandmother knocked on his door. "Sebastian dear, I'm making breakfast," she said through the door.

There was no answer.

*Oh God . . . oh God . . . oh God!*

She knocked again.

"He must be asleep, Gram. Leave him."

Her grandma turned and looked at her. "Katalina, what has gotten into you?"

"Just leave him!"

The door opened and Bass stepped out, dressed. "Did someone say breakfast?"

Katalina nearly collapsed to the floor in relief.

As they followed her grandma back toward the kitchen, Bass leaned toward Katalina, speaking in a voice so low only she could hear. "Shifter hearing, remember?"

*****

The morning flew by in a blur. Susan had finished sorting through paperwork and given Katalina's grandmother instructions. She was packing her things into her car while Katalina stood by the window, staring outside. She wasn't really watching her aunt, but staring off into the world, not taking anything in. Angry clouds filled the sky. They were growing by the minute. A wind had picked up, whipping her aunt's auburn hair around as she loaded her last suitcase.

Katalina thought the weather matched her mood. Her anger toward the universe and the fate she'd been given grew by the day. She knew it was only a matter of time until she reached her limit. Katalina wasn't sure what she'd do when that happened. She was no longer sure who she was; she was a shifter and yet she didn't feel like one at all. Yes, she was gifted with new senses and strengths, but they didn't feel like a part of her. She wasn't natural in her skin like Bass. She couldn't hear with the ears of a wolf without thinking; she wasn't fearless and brave.

Katalina felt like a stranger in her own skin, an imposter. She wasn't special. She was as ordinary as they came. She'd never been popular or the smartest in school. She'd just been Kat, the adopted kid with the strange hair. She'd give anything to turn back the clock and be that girl again, to have her parents and to feel safe, but she'd been living a borrowed life. It had never really been hers. She'd always been different, always been a shifter deep down. The problem was, she was now the strange kid in this new world. She still didn't belong. She was a shifter and yet she wasn't. She still felt like she was living a borrowed life.

"It's going to be okay, Katalina."

Katalina turned into Bass's embrace. She pressed her face into his chest and breathed in the wild scent of him.

"How do you know?" she whispered.

"Because I do. Do you trust me?"

Tilting her head up, she looked into his eyes. They were strong and fearless. "Yes," she answered.

"Then trust that everything will work out. That you'll end up where you're supposed to be, and one day, you'll be happy again. I still remember my mom, you know. I remember her smile and the way she used to tuck me into bed every night. I miss her every day. The part of my heart where she belonged will always be empty. The pain of her absence will always be there, but with time I've learned to live with my loss, to find the good in my life and hang onto it with all I've got. One day, it will get better. You just need to find the good to hang onto, to get you through."

Katalina tightened her hold and pressed her head back against his chest. *Find the good to hang onto.* She was hanging on and she never planned to let go.

Her aunt cleared her throat behind them. Reluctantly, Katalina pulled back, but she didn't let go of her grip on Bass's hand. "Are you going now?" she asked Susan.

"Yes, looks like a storm's coming in. I'd like to be on the road before it hits."

"Be careful."

Her aunt held out her arms for a hug, and Katalina felt like a little girl again as she went into them.

"I will, Kat. I'll see you soon, okay?" she murmured into Katalina's hair.

Katalina pulled back from the hug. "Tell Dillon I said hello."

Aunt Susan nodded at Katalina before her eyes rested on Bass, across the room. "It was nice to meet you, Bass. You be careful with this one's heart. It's been battered enough."

"I will," Bass replied, unfazed.

Katalina watched as her aunt walked out the door, her grandmother following behind, and a shiver of dread rolled down her spine. She wasn't quite sure what brought on the feeling, but then her wolf pushed against her skin, reminding her of who she now was. Her aunt was just going home. She'd see her again, but with each brush of fur, Katalina couldn't help thinking she didn't belong in this world anymore, no matter how hard she clung to it.

# CHAPTER 16

"Would you mind cutting some wood for me please, Sebastian?" Katalina's grandmother asked when she walked back inside. "That storm looks like it's going to be pretty nasty and we are nearly out."

"Not a problem at all."

Bass walked to the front door and slipped his feet inside his boots.

"Are you not going to put on a jacket, dear? It's pretty chilly out there."

Bass's hand paused on the door handle. He turned with a smile. "I'll be fine. I don't feel the cold."

Katalina followed him, putting her coat on as she passed the coat rack. She sat on a bench in the garden and watched him as he swung an ax over and over, the loud crack of wood splitting echoing around them. His lean muscles flexed beneath his tight sweater, his dark hair ruffled by the wind. Bass was all fine lines and chiseled muscle, a lethal wild animal wearing a civilized mask. Most people looked at Bass and saw a handsome young man with a warm smile and good manners, but Katalina saw all of him: the vulnerable boy who'd lost his mom, and the fierce, loyal wolf who lived, barely contained, beneath the surface.

She saw the smile he had only for her, and she'd witnessed the lines he'd crossed to protect her.

"What was it like growing up as a wolf?" she asked.

He didn't pause as he spoke, but his voice traveled over the sound of splitting wood. "Dark Shadow is an unforgiving pack. Only the strongest survive among them. It was hard. My father loved me but he didn't hold onto the good around him; he hung onto the pain. I remember the man he was, before my mother's death, and I know the man who raised me. Dark Shadow changed after such a loss and I don't think the pack ever recovered. I learned to fight at a young age. I learned that the people my age feared me. I learned to rely on only myself."

"That sounds awful," Katalina whispered, wanting to reach out and hold him, the pain in his voice physically hurting her.

"I didn't know any different, but I had my grandmother. My father's mother was kind and loving. She showed me the beauty of being a shifter. Shifters can be loyal creatures. When we love someone, we'll do everything in our power to make that person happy. It was hard growing up as a Dark Shadow, but I wouldn't change it."

"What about your mother's family?"

"My grandfathers died before I was born, both fighting, and my mother's mother went to sleep one day and never woke up. Her heart was broken from losing my mother."

"I think I'm pleased Jackson gave me away," she whispered, looking off into the distance.

Bass stopped, tossing the ax to the ground with a thud. "We could change the way things are."

"Is that what you want from me?"

"No, I just want to make you happy." He walked toward her, the love, the strength in his eyes too much for Katalina to bear. She glanced away, feeling unworthy. She was such a mess, her emotions all over the place, while Bass was so caring and understanding. He deserved someone who could accept who she was, someone who would run with him at night.

"I'm lost. I'm not sure who I am or what will make me happy," she admitted, looking down.

His hand grazed her jaw. "You'll find your way, and I'll be next to you every step of the way."

He walked toward the house, his arms full of wood.

"What about your home, Bass? Don't you miss your home, your grandmother?"

"She died last year. You're my home now, Katalina Winter."

Katalina sat for a long time outside on the bench. Bass walked back for wood a few times but never interrupted her. She wasn't thinking, not really. Her mind was a jumble of new information, questions with no answers, and questions with answers she didn't like. Her eyes stared off into the distance without taking in one particular thing.

The storm had made its way across the sky while she sat outside. Snow fell around her, thick and fast. It tangled in her hair and landed on her face, melting from the warmth of her skin. She stood, looking at the wonder around her. Her feet moved before she realized and her arms spread wide as she spun around. Her head tipped back to the sky and her coat flew out behind her as she laughed at her silliness. Katalina opened her eyes as she spun and noticed Bass watching. His hands tucked into the pockets of his jeans, he wore a breathtaking smile.

She stopped, his beauty causing her to fixate intently on him. How could someone so perfect, so loyal, belong to her?

*Find what makes you happy.*

Sebastian Evernight made her happy. She just wasn't sure she belonged in his world.

# CHAPTER 17

The storm outside passed but the storm inside Katalina only grew. The thought of Jackson sending more men made her so nervous she couldn't fully relax. She spent her days inside the house with Bass and her grandmother, avoiding the questions she wasn't ready to face yet.

Her grandmother tried to stay out of their way, knowing Katalina hadn't come to terms with everything. Gram had been packing things into boxes for the last few days, and it was something that Katalina tried not to focus on. She'd wanted nothing more than to escape Jackson's and go home, yet now she was beginning to see that it was the people who made a home, not the place, and her home was dead.

Most days rushed by in a blur. She felt adrift, struggling against an unforgiving current, only just keeping her head above the water. But then there was Bass, a constant presence keeping her breathing, holding her back from the inevitable fall.

She wanted to be with him, more than anything, but she knew deep down he didn't belong in this world she was clinging to. He was a wolf at heart, his spirit free; he belonged in the wilderness. He never said a word. He simply stayed by her side, as if he planned to live forever in Katalina's parents' house while sneaking out at night to let his wolf roam. Katalina had no answers. She wasn't sure if she could ever fully accept her wolf half, and she wasn't sure if she could live in the world Bass belonged to. Instead, she pushed the questions away, hiding and hoping that she'd never reach the point where she'd have a choice to make.

"Kat?" her grandmother said one morning.

"Hmm?" Katalina replied as she stuffed cereal into her mouth.

"I'm going to be gone for a night, two at most."

Katalina put down her spoon, turning to look at her grandmother. "Where are you going?"

"Well, I've got some items to take to Susan, and I want to store your parents' belongings at my house. I know I'm only an hour away but I'd rather stop overnight and rest."

"Why are you taking their things?" Katalina's heart raced, her skin turning clammy.

"Darling, I know you've been trying to ignore the fact that I'm packing up the house, but I can't afford to keep this house any longer than I have to. I need to have everything cleared and ready so I can put it on the market."

"You're selling straight away?" she asked in a small voice, feeling on the edge of a breakdown.

"I'm sorry. There is no other way. Kat, I'm worried about leaving you behind."

"I'll be fine!" she snapped, her fear of letting the past go clouding her judgment.

"Kat! I know none of this is fair, and I know you're not a child, but I still feel responsible for you, and I'm not sure your parents would have approved of you staying here alone with a boy."

It was all too much for Katalina. Her grandmother wanted to send Bass away. Bass, the one person keeping her from tumbling over the edge. "So this has nothing to do with me being upset my parents are dead!" she yelled, getting to her feet, trembling with anger. She wasn't even sure what she was angry at anymore; everything had just come to a point where she couldn't cope.

"Katalina, you know that's not what I meant."

She stood up, feeling overcome with rage. "I don't care what you think. This is my house until you sell it and I'm not leaving, and neither is Bass. I need him here." Katalina stormed out of the house, not bothering with a coat. She'd given up trying to pretend she was still an ordinary human. Everything was happening too fast. She needed to come to terms with their deaths. She needed the house to stay the same. She just needed one thing to stay the same, one thing to keep her in her old life.

Pain rippled through her body. She panted through it, her head pounding with each ragged beat of her heart. Sweat broke out over her skin as pain rippled through her again. She dropped to her knees, tears streaming down her face.

"Not now, not now! Go away, please . . . Please leave me alone . . ." she sobbed.

"Kat?" Bass was in front of her, his hands lifting her upright. "You can't change here, Kat. Come with me."

She pulled away. "No! I don't want to! I don't want this. Make it stop. Please, just make her go away."

She hated the pity that filled his eyes. She hated herself. Katalina wasn't ready to accept her wolf. She already had so much to come to terms with. There wasn't room for anything more.

"Katalina, you cannot keep denying who you are."

Katalina bit her lip and closed her eyes. She was so close to changing. She forced it back with all that she had. Her knees gave out, but Bass never let her fall. When she finally controlled her wolf, she was gasping for breath, soaked with sweat. She slumped against Bass, completely exhausted.

"Will you still love me if I never change again?" she whispered.

"I love every part of you, Katalina. Why don't you?"

*Because it's her fault. If she weren't a part of me, none of this would have ever happened.*

She couldn't say the answer out loud, maybe because she knew once she'd voiced it, she'd have to admit it wasn't her wolf's fault. But she had to blame someone; she had to channel her anger somewhere.

"Your grandmother is in your parents' room. She seems pretty upset, Kat. I think you should talk to her."

"I don't know what to say, Bass. It's not her fault. I know. I'm just not ready for any of this."

He tipped her chin up. "Katalina, would you have ever been ready for this?"

"Will you wait for me?" she asked, walking away from him into the house.

"Always." His soft voice wrapped around her like a shield. She could face this as long as she had him.

*Here goes nothing. Time to make things right.*

"Knock, knock," Katalina said, hoping to lighten the mood. Pushing the door open, she sucked in a ragged breath at the sight before her, trying to keep herself together. Her parents' room was full of boxes. The closet stood open, bare inside. Her mother's things had been packed away; jewelry, lotions, knickknacks—everything that made this room her parents', gone.

"I know it's a shock. I've just been packing nonstop. I thought if I didn't stop to really think about it, then it would never hit me."

Katalina smiled sadly, taking a seat on the end of the bed. "I'm sorry for before. I'm not sure how to cope with all of this, seeing everything of theirs, all of my home, packed into boxes. How is it ever going to be okay?"

Her grandmother sighed heavily. "It's not, Kat. I could have left everything as it was for years and it still wouldn't have been okay when I packed up their things. I don't want to do this, Kat, but I have no choice. The longer the house isn't sold, the less money you'll have to go to college with."

"College . . . I can't even think past today. How do I decide what I should be doing next year?"

"Kat, you don't have to decide anything now. Take a year off if you need to. Heaven knows you've been through hell. I'd be surprised if you figure out your next move any time soon, and that's okay, Kat. It's okay to feel lost and angry. Just don't let it be all you feel. Grief is a strange thing and it affects everyone differently. Give yourself time."

Katalina nodded. She looked around the room, each box tearing out another piece of her heart.

"I'm going to trust you here with Sebastian. I'm not sure where he fits in with all that's happened, but I can see he cares for you, and he seems to be the only thing keeping you from breaking. Please be careful, Kat. I couldn't bear to lose you, too."

"I will, don't worry." Katalina stood to leave; she'd had all she could take in her parents' room, which wasn't their room anymore.

"Oh, Kat?"

"Hmm?"

"That box there by the door, it's for you. I've put your mother's most treasured things in there. Well, apart from you anyway," Gram said with a smile. "She loved you more than anything. You know that, right?"

"Yes."

Katalina deposited the box in her room, saving it for the day she could open it. She found Bass outside where she'd left him. He turned at the sound of her approach. The smile he gifted her filled her with joy, and for just a second, she felt nothing but happiness.

"Can we go for a walk?"

"Sure."

Katalina threaded her arm through his waiting arm, leaning her head on his shoulder as they walked down the drive.

A bark came from behind her.

"Yes, you can come, too." She smiled at Arne as he bounded toward them.

"You don't have your coat on," Bass observed.

"I don't feel the cold like I used to. I guess it was habit. Plus, I thought my gram might notice if I suddenly started leaving it."

"So why leave it today?"

"I just didn't think about it. It's exhausting trying to remember how I used to be."

They walked in silence for a while. Katalina didn't really take in her surroundings. She clung to Bass and let him guide her along, listening only to the sound of their feet sinking into the snow. Arne ran in front of them, jumping around, digging at the snow. He ran up to Katalina and pressed his wet head against her legs. She patted his head, laughing, "Silly dog."

Suddenly her laughter died, as goose bumps broke out across her skin and a shiver ran down her spine.

Just as she was about to look behind her, Bass whispered, "Don't look. They've been following for a while."

"Do you think they'll attack?" she sighed, irritated.

"Not in the open."

"Maybe we should start heading back?"

"If you'd like."

They turned around, heading back down the road toward the house. "Come on, Arne," Katalina called, slapping her hand on her thigh. Arne paused, looking at the few trees in the distance.

"Here!" Bass growled.

With a whine, Arne put his head down and made his way over, looking sorry for himself. "No sulking, boy. You know what happens when you mess with wolves." Katalina ruffled his ears, cheering him up.

"Do you think Jackson will eventually just give up?" she asked hopefully.

"Sure, maybe."

Katalina glanced up at Bass. "If you're going to lie, lie better."

He smiled down at her. "I'll keep you safe." He kissed her forehead.

"I know," she replied.

*****

Katalina's grandmother left a few hours before dark, her car loaded with boxes. While Katalina was standing on the front step watching her drive away, Bass came up behind her, resting his head on her shoulder as his arms wrapped around her waist.

"I have you all to myself now. What wicked deed shall I do first?" He bit at her neck playfully.

"Oh, so now you show your true colors."

"I'm the big bad wolf, remember?"

"You're the shadow wolf," she smiled, turning her head to kiss his cheek.

"What makes you say that?" he murmured against her neck as he kissed and nipped at the sensitive skin.

Katalina shuddered, his onslaught of kisses turning her mind to mush.

"Katalina?"

"Hmm? Oh yeah . . . because when you stand in the shadows, it's as if they swallow you. You become a shadow yourself."

He turned her toward him, claiming her mouth with a demanding kiss. His hands made their way to her hips, branding her with his touch. Slowly, he guided her backward and into the house, never taking his mouth from hers.

Katalina's knees weakened when he touched and kissed her with such heat and possession. She was powerless to stop him and didn't want to.

"I think we should eat," he whispered, his mouth working its way across her jaw.

"Mmm . . ." was all Katalina could muster as a reply. She slipped her hands beneath his T-shirt, needing to feel his skin.

Bass pulled back, but Katalina held him tighter.

He chuckled against her mouth as she reached up on her toes and covered his mouth once again. "Food, Kat," he breathed into her mouth.

Katalina pulled back, breathless. "We'll get pizza delivered. Now, kiss me."

"Do they deliver this far out?"

Katalina sighed. "Yes, but they charge. Menu is by the phone."

He kissed her once more. "Go find something to watch while I order."

"Okay," she replied, reluctant to let Bass go.

They ate pizza and watched a movie, although they didn't actually watch much of the second half. Wrapped up in each other's arms, it was hard to concentrate on a film when all Katalina wanted was to lose herself in the feel of Bass.

# CHAPTER 18

Katalina woke with a start. The TV was still on, the start menu of the film filling up the screen. She sat up on the sofa, pulling the blanket off herself. "Bass?" she called, wondering where he was. Looking around the room, she spotted the half-eaten pizza. "Bass, are you here?" She stood.

She doubled over as a feeling of dread rolled through her. Katalina was running out the door before his name left her lips again. "Bass?"

She skidded to a stop outside the back door, the scene before her too horrifying to take in. Two wolves lay dead at the bottom of the garden. Bass was unmoving while another wolf tore at his flesh.

One instant she was running toward Bass, screaming, the next she was a wolf. A savage cry left her before she sank her teeth into the wolf. The two tumbled away, Katalina tearing at the wolf. The anger she'd been bottling up poured out of her. It was only when the wolf beneath her changed back to human that she stopped.

"Please, Kat, stop," the man before her gurgled as he choked on his blood.

Katalina changed back to human, her naked body covered in the blood of Jackson's enforcer.

"Tell Jackson if he ever sends someone after me again, I'll tell the police he kidnapped me, and if you ever attack me or Bass again, I *will* kill you!" She spoke each word slowly, her teeth gritted, her body trembling with anger.

Only when the enforcer nodded did she go to Bass. He'd changed back into his human form; blood covered half his body.

"Bass?" Katalina gasped, her anger washed away by bone-chilling fear. "Oh, God, please be okay."

She hooked her arms under his armpits, lifting him up, dragging him toward her house. She was stronger now, but Bass was so much larger than she was. It seemed to take an eternity to get him inside the house. She dragged him into her bedroom, lifting him as gently as possible onto the bed.

When she switched on the light, she saw the full extent of his injuries. His left side had been ripped to shreds, chunks of flesh missing. His shoulder was nothing but blood, his skin deathly pale. Katalina stumbled back, her hands covering her mouth as a strangled cry left her lips.

"Oh God . . . oh God . . . ambulance . . ." Her fingers shaking, she scrambled for the phone. The trembling in her hands traveled down her body until she could barely stand.

She picked up the phone and was about to dial the numbers when Bass's fingers brushed lightly against her leg. "No . . . no ambulance." His hand fell limp, fingers stained with a mixture of blood and dirt. She stared at his unmoving hand, her breathing rapid and broken. The phone fell from her grip, clattering to the floor. "Bass?" she whispered.

But he didn't answer her. The only sign he was still alive was the shallow rise and fall of his chest. Her knees gave out and her body trembled as she struggled to breathe. Lifting her head, she looked at the pale face of the boy she loved and dragged air into her lungs, forcing herself to calm down.

"Get yourself together, Kat. He needs you," she said to herself.

Drawing a lungful of oxygen inside her, she found the strength to stand. Giving Bass one last glance, she raced out of the room. Katalina found the medical kit and filled the largest bowl she could find with warm water.

Returning to her room, she saw that Bass hadn't moved. On her cream bedspread, his body was outlined in vivid crimson. Spreading the contents of the medical kit over the floor, Katalina growled in frustration. There was nothing for severe wounds. Swearing, she ran back out of the room and to the laundry cupboard, grabbing the nearest sheet she saw. She returned and began to cut and tear the sheet into strips.

As carefully as she could, Katalina used a dampened strip of sheet and cleaned his wounds as best she could, soon turning the bowl of water scarlet. Once she'd finished, she stood back and observed him, her shadow wolf, pale and broken.

She felt numb. The scene before her couldn't be real. How could her strong, wild wolf be injured? He was an untamed force, always ready to protect her.

*This is all my fault.* She looked at the various strips of sheet tied tightly around his middle, his shoulder a patchwork of gauze dressings.

*I've broken him, all to hold on to an impossible dream, a life that can never be mine again. Please be okay, Bass. Please hold on for me.*

Katalina slipped on Bass's abandoned shirt and, picking up a blanket, she climbed in the bed beside him. She left the clutter and chaos for the morning. At that moment, she was emotionally and physically drained. Curled up next to him, as close as she could without touching, she watched the shallow rise and fall of his chest, each breath a sign he was with her, that he was still holding on to life.

*****

"Kat?"

A brush against her side as light as a feather . . .

"K-Kat?"

Katalina gasped awake, shooting into a sitting position. Her eyes were wide with fear, her heart desperate to leap from her chest.

"Bass?" she whispered.

His eyes flickered open, the smallest of smiles appearing on his lips.

"Oh, thank God! I . . . I thought I was going to . . . lose you, too," she sobbed.

His fingers brushed lightly against hers. "Shifter, silly," he whispered.

"How do you feel? Can I get you anything?" she said in rapid fire, already out of bed and halfway to the door.

"Water . . ." he rasped.

Katalina ran from the room, filling a glass with water and retrieving a straw. She was back beside Bass within a minute, but when she returned, it was to find him asleep.

"Bass? Bass, your water," she said gently.

He didn't reply.

Katalina placed the water on the bedside table and cleaned her room. She only hoped her grandmother would stay away two nights, because she had no idea how she'd explain Bass being in bed injured and the two dead wolves in the garden.

*Garden.*

She raced to the back door, peering out through the tiny window. Early morning light filled the garden, making it seem blanketed in a gray haze, but even in the dim light, Katalina could see there were no longer wolf bodies littering the bottom of her garden. She double-checked the locks before returning to Bass. By the time she'd cleared her bedroom floor of all the evidence from the night before, he'd woken again.

"Thanks," he whispered after she helped him take a drink.

She smiled, putting the glass down, afraid if she opened her mouth to speak the tears inside would come spilling out.

"Kat, go get a shower. I'll still be here when you get out," he said, his voice clearer since drinking.

She shook her head. "I'm fine."

"Baby, you've got blood on your face."

She lifted a trembling hand to her face. Glancing at Bass, she left the room as quickly as she could without actually breaking into a run.

While the bathroom filled with steam, Katalina unbuttoned Bass's shirt that she'd thrown on last night and dared a quick glance in the mirror. There were smudges of mud and blood across her forehead. Her hair was a matted mess and a glance at her feet confirmed she'd run outside with nothing on but an old T-shirt and jeans. Those clothes were gone now, destroyed as she'd changed into her wolf.

The stream of hot water was a welcome sensation. The tension and worry washed from her body, along with the mud and blood staining her skin. It took two applications of shampoo to wash the knots from her hair, but by the time she stepped out of the shower, she felt clean and new.

"Shit . . . clothes," she mumbled, looking at the dirty shirt discarded on the floor.

Taking a deep breath, she stepped from the bathroom and padded quietly toward her bedroom. With any luck, Bass would be asleep and not notice her walking around in just a towel, but when her door opened, his eyes fluttered open, locking on her. Katalina knew she was being silly. He'd seen her naked a number of times, but this felt different. She'd just come from the shower. She didn't have the confidence to just drop her towel and act as if she were brave.

She froze, gripping the edge of the towel tighter. "I forgot clothes," she squeaked, ready to die from embarrassment.

He smiled at her. "I've seen it all before," he said quietly, still sounding weak.

"This is different, Bass. I . . . I'd just been a wolf. The last thing on my mind was being naked and having you check me out."

She turned her back to him, rummaging in her wardrobe for something easy to slip on.

"I feel like a complete dick now because I was definitely checking you out, all naked and beautiful in my arms."

She spun around to face him, her face heating. The light had returned to his eyes, the smile on his lips wicked and playful. "You, Sebastian Evernight, are a bad, bad wolf!" she said in mock outrage.

"And you, Katalina Winter, look adorable when mad. Come here so I can kiss that look from your lips."

"No! I can't believe you were looking at me," she huffed, grabbing the nearest dress in her wardrobe and pulling it over her head. She wiggled the towel out from underneath.

"Come on, Kat. I couldn't help it! I'm a man after all. Come here. I'd come to you, but it appears I'm not as indestructible as I thought."

*No, you're not.* She looked from one injury to the next. With a heavy sigh, Katalina perched lightly on the edge of the bed. "I thought you were going to die. What happened last night?" she asked tentatively, still shaken from the night before.

"My wolf was antsy, so I thought I'd slip out for a run while you were sleeping. But in my haste to return to you, I didn't notice Jackson's men waiting for me. They jumped me. The first went down easily, the second not so much. From there, it's all a bit of a blur."

"You'd taken two out when I got to you, but the third"—a shudder rolled through her—"you didn't even move. I was so mad, so frightened. There was no chance of me controlling my wolf. One minute I was me, the next . . ."

He lifted an unsteady hand to gently caress her cheek. "You saved me."

"It scares me, Bass . . . being a wolf."

"Why?"

"Because this wolf, this animal inside me . . . she's wild, untamed. What happens when I like what she makes me?"

He looked at her for a very long time. For a moment, Katalina thought he wasn't going to answer her. However, the look in his eyes said he would. He just needed to find the right words.

"Do you think I'm a monster?"

"What? No!"

"Then why would you think you'd be one? When I'm a wolf, life becomes simpler, but I'm not two people. Being a shifter doesn't mean you have a nice side and a bad side. You've always been a shifter, Kat. You'd just never changed. Your wolf has always been in here." He placed his hand over her heart. He continued, "She's not a monster. She's wild and free, but no monster. We don't kill for the sake of killing. At the heart of who we are, we are loyal. Nothing comes before those we love."

She swallowed the tears blocking her airway. She didn't know how to reply. She opened her mouth, unsure of the words that would spill out. "I need you to get better, Bass. I'm holding on, but . . . but my grip . . . it's faltering."

He smiled sadly at her. "One day, you'll see what I see. One day, you'll be shocked by the realization of how strong you actually are."

Katalina curled into a ball on the bed beside him. She felt exposed to the world, the grip on her sanity wavering. Bass wrapped an arm around her, and with a shaky breath, she hoped he was enough to keep her tethered.

# CHAPTER 19

Katalina didn't do much else that day. She slept for a while next to Bass, and only left him to throw a stick for Arne. Standing on the threshold, Katalina threw the stick out onto the drive, and waited for Arne to return it to her. Every once in a while, he'd stop and whine, staring off into the distance.

"I know, boy. I'm sorry, but it's not safe out there." She didn't even feel especially safe standing on the porch. She kept her hand on the door, ready to slam it shut if anyone came near her. She wondered if Jackson would give up since he'd lost two of his men. Did the one she attacked make it back with her message? Was it Jackson who'd left her garden empty of all evidence?

The phone rang.

"Arne! Come on!" She slapped her leg frantically, trying to get him to move faster. "Move it!" He sauntered inside, not at all bothered by the phone ringing.

Katalina slammed the door shut, threw the dead bolt across, and raced for the phone.

"Hello?" she said breathlessly.

"Kat? It's me. Why are you so out of breath?" It was Gram.

"I was outside with Arne, had to run. Are you on your way back?" *Please say no. Please say no.*

"No, sorry. I've just arrived at your aunt's. I'm going to spend some time with Dillon, stay the night, and set off tomorrow afternoon."

"Okay." She remembered too late she shouldn't sound so cheerful.

"Katalina, is everything okay there? You are being careful, right?"

"Everything's great, Gram. Don't worry."

Her grandmother paused for a second. "You're taking precautions, right? I know you are eighteen now, and well, he's a nice boy."

*OH MY GOD!*

"Gram, stop! S-stop!" she stuttered into the phone. A wave of embarrassment heated her cheeks.

"I've got to say these things now, Kat. I'd love for your mother to be here, but . . . I know what young people get up to. I used to be young once myself. Hard to believe, I know—"

Katalina cut off her words, wanting the floor to open up and swallow her. "STOP! I'm a virgin, Grandma. We do not need to have this conversation. We NEVER need to have this conversation, so stop, okay? Stop before I can never look you in the eyes again."

"Oh—well, okay, dear, I'll see you tomorrow then."

"Bye, Gram."

She put down the phone and stood shell-shocked for a moment before Arne knocked against her knees.

"Can you believe she said that?" she muttered to the dog.

"You do realize he can't understand you, even though you are a shifter."

Katalina's head shot up. "Get back in bed!" she snapped, pointing a finger.

"No . . . don't make me. I'm going to go insane if I lie there any longer."

"Fine. Sofa." She pointed with one hand; the other rested on her hip.

"Did I ever tell you, you are hot as hell when bossing me about?"

Her stern face slipped. She fixed it quickly but he saw.

"Stop being a smart-ass and sit down."

"Can I get some food?" he asked, lowering himself to the sofa so slowly Katalina couldn't watch.

*All your fault, all your fault . . .*

She willed the voice in her head to shut up.

"I fed you an hour ago."

"My body's burning more fuel so I can heal faster."

*All your fault . . .* There was that voice again, taunting her, reminding her he was injured because she couldn't let go.

"I think we have some chips and a pizza in the freezer?"

"Your culinary skills never cease to amaze." He flashed her a wicked smile.

Katalina stuck out her tongue and turned quickly on her heel so he wouldn't see the smile on her face. She loved that he showed her this side. This Bass was fun, playful, and a little mischievous. She wondered how many people saw more than the intense, logical Sebastian Evernight. Smiling, she opened the freezer and secretly wished that this Bass were hers alone.

Bass ate the whole pizza, except for one slice Katalina nibbled. He was asleep minutes after finishing, the TV on but unwatched. Katalina sat on one end of the sofa with Bass's legs across her, trapping her in. She reached for a book that had been left on the lamp table. Her mother's bookmark still marked the place she'd read up to.

Although she didn't read romance novels often, Katalina had to do something. The TV didn't hold her interest and simply sitting was a dangerous thing; her mind would wander, going to the places she wasn't ready to go. She left the bookmark on the page it had marked; the thought of losing her mother's place made her stomach churn and twist uncomfortably. Turning to the first page, Katalina left her world for a little while, knowing reality would soon come calling.

*****

Katalina's grandmother was due to arrive back in less than an hour. Katalina's nerves were high. She felt jittery and unsafe within her own skin.

"Katalina, will you please sit? Your pacing is making me nervous, and I am not the kind of person who gets nervous!"

Katalina paused to glare at Bass. He sat on the sofa chair, flicking through channels, looking bored and sexy at the same time. He didn't look nervous. She wondered if he ever got nervous, or feared anything.

"I can't help it. I feel . . . I feel like I'm going to jump out of my skin. It's like I can feel disaster approaching. She's going to notice you're hurt, and then there's Jackson. How long can I possibly forget he exists?"

Bass gave her a sad smile. Getting to his feet, he attempted to hide his pain, but she saw it: that split second when his mask slipped.

"How much pain are you really in?" she asked.

"I'm—"

She cut him off. "Do not lie to me!"

"All right, it has been a while since I have been as injured as I am, but Katalina, I really need you to stop worrying. I'm going to heal. My shoulder will be fine by the morning."

"And your stomach?"

"Few days at most."

"I just feel . . . feel so responsible." Instantly, she felt better for sharing.

"Baby"—he hugged her gently—"I volunteered to bring you here, remember? No one makes me do anything. This is what you needed, and I am in the business of giving you what you need."

"What about what you need, Bass? I've been so selfish."

Bass let her go and walked away. While settling himself onto the sofa, he couldn't keep the grimace from his face. "Will you stop blaming yourself for everything?" he growled.

Katalina sighed. "If I don't hate myself, who do I hate?"

"Do you know what you need, Kat? You need to be a wolf."

"What?"

"Strip off. Summon the change. It will do you good. Your brain needs a reset; being a wolf, if only for a little while, will do that."

"I can't go outside. It might not be safe . . . Someone could see me."

"Change in here then. Just escape that mind of yours, which seems insistent on torturing itself."

She frowned at him, about to argue.

"For once, will you just do as I say?"

He sounded tired, exhausted from life. She hated it. Hated that he'd lost the fighting spirit that she loved about him and was familiar with.

"Okay." Katalina disappeared into her bedroom and stripped off her clothes.

Taking a deep breath, she thought of her wolf, willing her to take over. Pain snatched away all thought as her body snapped and broke, changed and mended. One minute she was human, head full of thoughts, and the next she was nothing but scent, sound, and wolf.

She padded out on paws, seeing her house through new eyes (the fibers of the carpet and the tiny flecks of dust drifting through the air), scents (sweet and acid), and sounds (the mumble of the TV, the distant call of a bird, the far-off hum of traffic). She was wild, her mind free of stress or worry and the burden of guilt.

Katalina explored the house before heading toward Bass. She wanted to focus on only him. His scent filled her nose while his heat warmed her fur. Through her blood their connection pumped, a wild, beautiful thing.

"Hello, my gorgeous winter wolf," Bass murmured softly, pressing a kiss to her head. "Someday soon, we are going to run together again."

His words conjured up an image: the night of her first change. She could almost touch the memory, feel the wind in her fur, the scents all around her. Images of Bass tumbled across her mind. Her shadow wolf, dangerous and beautiful, fierce and loving, he was everything to her wolf, the purpose of her being. And then she remembered the first time she'd seen him—but it was a human memory rather than a wolf one. The change back to her human self came naturally, as if shaking off a coat.

"You knew, didn't you? The first day we met, you knew who I was to you."

A glint in his eyes and the smile on his face did funny things to her heart. "Of course I did."

"Why did you know and I didn't?"

"I think you did, really, deep down in the part of you locked away."

She remembered how she felt the moment he left, the hollowness and the sudden, desperate urge to follow him.

"You acted so cool, so indifferent. *You intrigue me, Katalina Winter.*" She laughed at her attempt to mimic him.

"You do intrigue me."

"I hope it's a little more than that?"

"Oh, so much more," he said, his voice a rough caress as his eyes heated with desire.

Remembering she was naked, Katalina became self-conscious. She looked down at herself, crouched by his legs, just as her wolf had been. Her wolf took over once more.

"No fair," Bass whined, but the cheeky smile on his face gave him away.

Katalina nipped at him and gave him a playful growl before running off to her bedroom. She returned minutes later, dressed and feeling a little less crazy.

"Better?"

"Yes."

"Good, because I hear a car coming."

Katalina angled her head to listen, and sure enough, she heard the distant purr of an engine and the crunch of gravel as the car turned into her drive.

She let out a long, low breath, shaking her hands before facing the door.

"Kat, you look like you're about to announce to your grandmother that you're pregnant, or running away. Go do something."

She shook her head, smiling at herself. "I think I may have damaged my head in that accident." She headed into the kitchen to put on the kettle.

"Wonderful. I get to live with a brain-damaged mate for the rest of my life." His laugh rumbled toward her.

"You can't talk. You don't even live in the real world!"

"Tell me, Katalina, what is it you do in this real world?"

"You know, lots of things: Facebook, Twitter, see a movie."

"I went to the movies once."

Katalina came out of the kitchen, a look of disbelief on her face. "Once?"

"Yes, once, when I was a child, with my grandmother."

Katalina shook her head sadly. "I'm afraid there is no hope for you."

"I'd like to see this real world, Katalina. Will you show me?"

"It would be my pleasure, but you must show me how you disappear into the shadows."

He laughed at her. "I don't disappear, Kat. I'm just camouflaging myself. You may find it difficult with white fur . . ." His sentence trailed off as the door opened.

"Gram, I just put on the kettle. Do you want some tea?" Katalina called, heading back into the kitchen.

"That would be wonderful, darling."

# CHAPTER 20

As night fell and her grandmother remained unsuspecting of Bass's injuries, Katalina wondered what she'd been so worried about.

"Well, dear, I'm going to bed."

"Me too. Night, Kat." Bass kissed her on the cheek before getting to his feet and walking off to his room. She knew he wouldn't spend the night in there, even though she'd told him not to sneak around injured.

"Night." Katalina gathered the mugs and took them into the kitchen.

Arne whined and scratched at the door.

"Hold on, boy. Let me wash these," Katalina called from the kitchen.

"I'll let him out, Kat," her grandmother replied.

Katalina turned on the tap. She heard the sound of the lock turning and Arne's paws as he bounded over the wooden porch, followed by his bark as he chased whatever prey he'd found.

She switched the tap off.

Silence.

Her feet were moving before her wolf senses kicked in, but she knew even before she saw him: Jackson had come for her.

Her grandmother stood in shocked silence, her back pressed against the wall. Jackson's eyes locked with Katalina's. She was expecting terror, or even the slightest lingering of fear, but all she felt was pure, white-hot rage.

"OUT!" she yelled at the man who'd made her, yet had no right to claim the title *father*.

Bass was beside her a moment later. "Katalina, calm down," he whispered.

But it was too late for that. She'd been bottling her rage, her sorrow, and her confusion for too long and now it burst from her like a raging storm, savage and unrelenting.

"I said GET OUT!" Her eyes glanced at Arne, who lay unmoving in the snow. "What did you do?"

Jackson looked behind him. "Oh, he'll be—" His words blew out of him, along with his breath. Katalina was shocked by how far he stumbled from her push, but it didn't stop her attack. She screamed as she hit him. He fell back, hitting the porch with a thud, looking at her in complete shock.

"How dare you!" Jackson rumbled, his eyes flashing with anger.

His words only enraged her more. She went as if to leap onto him but found arms pinning her back.

"Katalina, no!" Bass's words didn't reach her. She could think of nothing but ripping Jackson to shreds. "Kat, please." Bass trapped her against the wall.

Katalina felt the roll of pain signaling the change, her body shuddered.

"Kat, stop!" Jackson growled. She felt the power of the alpha in his voice, but she brushed it off, a scream converting to a snarl ripping from her throat.

"You can't control me!" she spat, her body trembling. Disregarding what her grandmother—who still stood frozen against the wall—thought, she couldn't think beyond the red haze of anger.

"Kat, look at me!"

Katalina glanced at Bass, his voice strained, sweat covering his forehead. She stopped struggling immediately. She was hurting him, but it didn't stop her wolf from wanting out, from wanting to sink teeth into Jackson. She shook her head, her hands and her skin on fire. Her body felt too tight. This mask needed to come off; she needed to let her wolf out.

"Not now, Katalina," Bass whispered to her.

"I . . . I can't control it." Her skin broke out in sweat, breathing became difficult; she was so close to changing, so close to revealing who she really was.

"Yes, you can. Look at me, Katalina. Look at me. Feel me."

His voice was low and hypnotic. Staring into the endless depths of his starlit eyes, she relaxed. Where once had been anger, there was love; his feelings ran through her, breaking the hold of her wolf. She let out a shuddering breath, ready to face Jackson.

"You need to leave." She said each word slowly.

Jackson's eyes darted from Bass to her. "What have you done?" he yelled, stepping back inside the house. "I'll kill you for this!" he threatened.

Katalina was trembling again. She took a step toward Jackson. "I said LEAVE! Leave before you do even more damage!"

"I-I think you should do as she says . . . Or-or I'll call the police," her grandmother stammered, looking frightened.

Katalina was a tight ball of anger, ready to uncoil and spring at a second's notice. She stared unblinking at Jackson, feeling the unease within him grow.

"You shouldn't be able to do that. I'm your alpha," Jackson said to Katalina in disbelief. He was right—as an alpha, his command should have stuck, but Katalina had never viewed Jackson this way.

"No. You. Are. Not!"

He looked at her a second longer before backing out of the door. Katalina's grandmother rushed to shut it but his arm blocked the way.

"Regardless of what you think of me, Katalina, we do need to talk. Whether you want to address our issues or not, it's not safe here for you anymore."

When Katalina didn't answer, he removed his arm and vanished into the night.

They all stood in silence, staring at nothing.

"Arne!" Katalina gasped, rushing for the door.

"Kat, he might still be out there. Shall we call the police?" Her grandmother looked as white as a sheet.

"He's gone, Gram. Go sit down."

She rushed toward her dog. "Arne," she whispered, her hands lightly touching him.

"Is he breathing?"

Kat looked up over her shoulder. Bass stood protectively over her, his eyes darting one way and the next.

"Y-yes."

"I can't smell blood. Pick him up and take him inside."

Katalina did as he said. He followed her, a constant, watchful presence.

The moment her grandmother saw them, the questions started. "Katalina, who was that? What did he want? What does he mean, it's not safe? I don't understand any of this . . . Why were you so mad, Kat? I've never seen you that way."

Katalina and Bass's eyes locked.

"He's my biological father," she answered with her back to her grandmother.

"Father?" she whispered.

There were a few more moments of silence while her grandmother thought.

"That was the man who found you? I don't understand. Why was he so angry?"

Katalina looked at Bass for help.

"Jackson doesn't like my family very much," Bass said.

"But then why—"

"Look, Gram, it's complicated. Please, enough with the questions." Katalina turned to Bass. "Do you think I should call a vet, Bass?"

"Katalina, he said you weren't safe."

"He's full of shit!" she snapped.

"Katalina!" her grandmother gasped, outraged.

Katalina jumped to her feet. "I. Do. Not. Have. Time. For. This. I'm taking him to the vet. Bass, grab the keys!"

Katalina stormed out the house, her unconscious dog in her arms. She didn't pause to see if Bass was coming; he had no choice. This was not open for debate.

# CHAPTER 21

Katalina felt years older by the time the vet approached her. She'd been pacing the small waiting room for an hour. Bass sat in silence, his eyes following her relentless walking.

"Oh, thank God. Is he all right?" she asked, turning to face the vet.

"Yes, he's going to be fine. Seems to have been knocked unconscious, but I'd like to keep him overnight for observation, just in case."

"Okay. Can I see him?"

"I've given him a light sedative. He should rest, so I'll call you tomorrow when I have some more news."

"Okay, thank you." Katalina reluctantly left the vet's office, Bass following behind. "I'm driving."

Bass threw the keys to Katalina. She caught them a few inches from her face.

"Wow, I'm not sure I'm ever going to get used to these reflexes."

They drove in silence for a while, the roads dark and deserted.

"How badly did I hurt you?" she asked quietly.

"The wound's split back open from trying to hold you back, but it's nothing to worry about. I'll soon be back to full strength."

"I should have left you at the vet's. You and Arne could have been cage neighbors," she joked.

"Hmm, I'm not sure I find your joke very funny."

"Oh, come on, Bass. Lighten up! It's been one hell of a night."

"I'd have to agree with you there," he answered, sounding tired.

As she pulled into her drive, Katalina voiced her realization, the one she'd had for some time but hadn't wanted to accept for fear of what it might bring.

"It's time I went back," she sighed.

"I know," he murmured, linking his hand with hers.

"How long were you going to pretend we could live here? Playing the role of suburban wolf?" She turned off the truck, plunging them into darkness.

"For as long as you needed, Katalina."

"What did I ever do to deserve you?"

"We're going to get through this, you know," Bass said quietly.

"How can you be so sure? I don't fit in your world. I'm not sure I fit anywhere."

"I never fit in my world either, Kat. We are going to make a new world, just for us."

"Can we face this new world tomorrow, after some sleep?"

Bass's laugh filled the dark truck. "Sure, Kat."

*****

Katalina expected to toss and turn that night, but the moment she slid into bed, her exhaustion took over. Bass climbed in behind her, pulling her close. She slept in his embrace and woke feeling refreshed and ready to tackle life head-on.

"Packing already?" Bass asked.

Katalina smiled at him. He was in her bed, his chest bronzed and bare.

"Are you checking me out, Katalina Winter?" he asked with a wicked smile when she didn't answer his first question.

She dragged her eyes away.

"It's what we do in the real world."

"I am liking this real world quite a lot. Maybe you should get changed, so I can do some checking out of my own."

"Bass!" Katalina hissed. "My gram is down the hall. Maybe you should get up?" She tried to hide the silly grin on her face.

"It's six a.m., Kat. Can't I lounge for a little while longer? I am injured."

"Fine, I need tea. Do you want some coffee?"

"Coffee in bed? Now, this I could get used to."

"Don't push your luck, Sebastian, or the real world might throw you back."

She returned five minutes later, two mugs in hand. She sat cross-legged at the end of her bed, sipping tea.

"How's the stomach? Let's see."

"If you want to see me naked, all you have to do is ask."

Katalina shook her head at the wicked glint in his eyes. "I think you've been in the real world too long. Can I have the straitlaced, serious Sebastian Evernight back?"

"I've never been straitlaced," he answered, pulling the duvet down to reveal his wound.

Placing her mug on the bedside table, Kat untied the strips of sheet around his middle and pulled them off. "Wow!" she breathed. "I honestly thought you were going to die when I saw this a few days ago."

"Perks of being a wolf."

"I'll go get a dressing. I think there's a big one left."

Katalina stuck the dressing on his stomach, her fingers brushing over warm skin. She found them wandering on their own, tracing each curve of his abs; steadily, they made their way up to his chest. Hands splaying possessively, she looked up to see eyes of starlit night, hungry with desire.

Their breathing shallow and hearts beating rapidly, they remained locked in each other's gaze.

She was in his lap a second later, forgetting he was hurt, forgetting everything but him. His hands explored her body as if she were a piece of art. Lingering on the curve of her hip, the edge of her rib, his hands held her possessively. She crushed her lips to his, wanting and consuming, pouring into him everything she felt, every kiss saying *I love you . . . I love you . . . I love you . . .*

The creak of a door and the shuffle of feet broke them apart in a gasp for air, chests heaving and hearts booming.

"Hide!" Katalina hissed as her hearing picked up the sound of feet coming toward her door.

"Kat?" Her grandmother knocked softly on the door.

Kat glanced back at her bed, but Bass had gone. *How does he move so silently?*

"Yeah?"

"Hey—oh, are you going somewhere?" Her grandmother glanced at her bed, sheets and duvet rumpled, and her duffle bag, half-open, with clothes spilling out of it.

"Yeah, I need to go talk to Jackson."

"Is that wise? He seems like a very angry man."

Katalina sighed. Dropping the clothes from her hand, she slumped on the bed.

"The thing is, Gram, he is my father, and I need to see this through. I know he's an arrogant ass and has a serious temper, but I need to hear him out."

"Did you meet your mother as well, Kat?"

"No, I . . . she's . . . she's dead. She was murdered when I was a baby. That's why Jackson gave me away. I guess he couldn't handle me after he lost his wife."

"Murdered? Gosh, Kat, that's terrible."

Katalina nodded, unsure what to say.

"Look, Kat, I can't tell you what to do. Only you can decide what is best, but I want you to know you owe that man nothing. He may be your biological father but he gave up every right the day he left you on our doorstep."

"I know, Gram. I just want to sort things out between us so I can move on."

"You'll call me when you arrive? Where is it you're going?"

"Up north near Atlanta—he has a farm out there. It's pretty remote."

"You will keep in touch? There'll always be a place for you at my house. Susan and I, we'll always be your family. You do know that, right?"

"Of course, Gram." Katalina hugged her.

"Oh, I forgot to ask: How's Arne?"

"They kept him in for observation. The vet is going to call this morning, but she thought he was going to be fine."

"Oh, that's good then. Are you taking him with you?"

"Yes. I'm not leaving without him."

Her gram got up to leave, pausing at the door. "I'm just going to run to the store for milk."

"Drive safely," Katalina smiled.

Once the door closed, Bass walked out of her wardrobe. His shorts hung low on his waist. Katalina was too distracted by his raw male beauty to notice the dress he held.

"You should pack this. I like it."

*What?* "Oh, that. Read the tag," she said with a smile.

Bass read the words on the tag pinned to the dress:

*Be my summer girl.*
*—Dad*

"Summer girl?"

"I don't like shopping. Hate it, in fact. Either Mom or Dad bought most of the clothes in my wardrobe. Mom had a thing for buying me anything white or wintery, whereas Dad always bought me summer dresses, which I hardly ever wear. I'm more a shorts and T-shirt kind of girl. Dad bought that for Christmas. I haven't worn it yet."

"Definitely packing it then." Bass scrunched it up and stuffed it, along with the hanger, in her bag.

Katalina pulled it out with a huff, removing the coat hanger and folding the dress neatly. "You do know it's winter and there's a foot of snow on the ground?"

"So? I'm going to look forward to the first day of summer." He stalked slowly toward her, the edge of his mouth lifting in a delicious way. "Then you can be my summer girl." His lips crushed hers, and for the next twenty minutes Katalina accomplished nothing but thoroughly kissed swollen lips.

"I really need to pack!" She eventually swatted him away as he tried to pull her back. "Go pack your own stuff."

"I brought a backpack. It will take me all of ten seconds."

"Go make some food then. Do something other than distract me."

Katalina picked a box up, heading outside for the truck. Bass swiped for her bottom, his fingers brushing across her cheek as she jumped away with a squeal.

"Leave me alone," she giggled, opening the front door one-handed while balancing the box on her knee. Distracted, she didn't sense the person lurking outside, waiting to grab her.

"Kat!" Bass gasped too late.

She'd half turned back when a hand closed over her mouth and the sharp edge of a knife pressed against her throat.

The box fell from her grip as the intruder pushed her flush against the wall. With wide eyes, she stared at the young man holding her. His ash-blond hair was styled into a messy flick. His green eyes held a look of danger but also mischief, and his smile said he was having the time of his life.

"Now tell me, how's a pretty thing like you keeping the alpha's son locked up?"

"NICO! I'm not locked up. Please take the knife from my mate's throat," Bass said sharply.

"Mate?" Nico let out a loud, cheeky laugh. "Oh Bass, this is the best move you've ever pulled!"

"She's not a move, Nico!" Bass growled.

"Doesn't matter. Your dad's going to be so pissed! Can't wait to see you talk your way out of this one."

Katalina cleared her throat, glaring at Nico.

"Oh, right, yes. Sorry 'bout that." He peeled his hand from her mouth and removed the knife as he stepped back.

"I'm Nico. Nice to meet ya." He pulled her in for a hug. Bass growled at the contact.

"Oh, chill!"

Katalina stood speechless. She couldn't imagine this boy growing up in the same place as Bass.

"So, are you always this quiet?" Nico asked, the larger-than-life smile still on his face.

"What? Oh, no—I'm Kat."

"Nico, why are you here?" Bass interrupted, taking a step forward, positioning himself between Nico and Katalina.

"Your dad's on the warpath, Bass. He's saying River Run has you. He knows it's not true, but he's using it as an excuse, gearing everyone up for attack. Your scent's all over their land, but I couldn't see you. Then their alpha returned. Fuming, he was. I heard him shouting about you and her." He nodded toward Katalina. "I talked one of the enforcers into telling me the address of this place and came looking."

"Has he sent anyone out to scout for my whereabouts?"

"No, he doesn't give a shit. Just wants blood. That's all he's ever wanted and you're giving him a pretty good excuse. I think you best get your ass home!"

"I can't, not yet."

"Might be too late now. He's rounded up a few people willing to attack without proof of your capture. Honestly, Bass, River Run has no chance. They've a few good fighters, but I saw one guy return cut to hell. He had two others dead in his truck. They have those two brothers; the younger one is a hell of a fighter, but pitch a few adults against him and, well . . ."

Katalina listened to every word as they poured in a rush from Nico's mouth. The more he said, the sicker she felt. Here she was worrying about herself, wanting desperately to get away from Jackson, and now she'd brought them more trouble. She swallowed the lump in her throat and reached out for Bass.

"We need to go." Her voice was quiet.

Bass wrapped his hand around Katalina's waist, pulling her to his side. "Kat, don't worry. We're going back. Everything will be fine."

"How do you know that? What about your father?"

"I'll think of something," he said quietly, pressing a kiss to her cheek.

"Don't worry, Kat. Bass is the master of talking himself out of shit! His dad hates it. He'll scream and shout, and Bass never rises. He voices his opinion and walks away."

Katalina shook her head at Nico. The boy seemed to love drama. "I can't imagine you being a rebel, Bass."

"I'm not a rebel. I just have very different views from my father and I'm not frightened to tell him."

"Yeah, keep telling yourself that, Bass," Nico laughed.

"Make yourself useful, Nico. Go back home and try to stall my father. I'll be there soon."

"Sure thing, Bass. See ya again, Kat." He flashed her a mischievous smile before walking away.

The phone started to ring, so Katalina ran for it.

"Hey, wait up a sec, Nico," she heard Bass shout before she picked up the phone.

*****

Katalina put down the phone, feeling happier that Arne was on the mend and that she could pick him up. She turned to head for her bedroom when she heard Bass talking.

"I need to know you've got my back."

"Sure, man, but I'm sure it won't come to that."

"Nico, I'm not sure I can talk myself out of this one."

"You really willing to take on your own dad?"

"I'll do whatever it takes to keep her safe."

Katalina ran for her bedroom. She randomly grabbed clothes from her drawers and wardrobe, not bothering to fold them. Her stomach churned uncomfortably; dread, like a living thing, clawed its way through her veins. She'd made up her mind: they were leaving now, and the sooner they were back on pack lands, the sooner she could fix this mess.

# CHAPTER 22

Katalina sipped her way through one last cup of tea with her grandmother before hitting the road. The truck was packed. A suitcase full of random clothes and a few boxes of her things were strapped down in the back of Bass's truck.

"I'll take the rest of your things to my house for when you need them, Kat," her grandmother said quietly, unsure of Katalina's reaction.

"Yep," she answered, trying to sound more positive than she felt.

"Have you heard from the vet?"

"Yeah, he's going to be fine. We'll get him before we go. The vet said he just has to take it easy for a few days."

"Now, you make sure to drive safely with my granddaughter as your cargo, Sebastian."

"Yes, ma'am. I'll take good care of Katalina, don't you worry."

"I'm not worried. Kat is a strong young woman. She'll do just fine taking care of herself."

Katalina smiled at her grandmother over her mug. *I sure hope you're right, Gram.*

Saying farewell to her grandmother and the house she'd grown up in was a lot harder than Katalina had anticipated. Sure, she wanted to be back at Jackson's making sure Toby and Cage were okay, but a part of her still wasn't ready to let go of her old life. Leaving this time was final. She'd always have a home with her grandmother or aunt, but she had to say good-bye to this house—her home. She glanced one last time at the house before climbing into the truck. She pictured her smiling, happy parents standing beside her grandmother, waving.

Tears welled in her eyes. "Good-bye, Mom, Dad," she whispered. "I love you."

Swallowing her grief, she breathed in one last gulp of fresh winter air and entered the truck, slamming the door behind her.

"Drive, Bass, before I change my mind and hide in that house forever."

The truck rumbled to life and made its way down the drive. Bass pulled out onto the road, passed the spot where her life had changed irrevocably, and drove her away. Unable to hold in her tears, Katalina pulled her knees up to her chest, silently crying as she watched the world flash by. Bass's hand linked with hers. It was strong and warm, a constant reminder she wasn't alone, and never would be again.

They picked up Arne and headed away from Detroit, the drive up I-75 a quiet one. Bass seemed happy with the silence, and Katalina was grateful; she didn't know what to say to him. She was also frightened that if he did break the silence, she might ask him the question that had been spinning around and around inside her mind.

*What did "I'm not sure I can talk myself out of this one," mean?*

What was he willing to do to keep her safe? The problem was, deep down she already knew the answer, and she wasn't sure she liked it: *Anything.*

*****

167

"Hey, Kat." Bass's fingers stroked hair from her face. "Baby, we're nearly there. Do you want to stretch your legs?"

"Mmm, sure." She stretched her arms up and yawned. "Come on, boy. Let's take a walk," she said, scratching Arne behind the ear.

Katalina walked Arne along the edge of the parking lot away from the gas station. Tall trees towered above her. They'd left suburbia far behind. The landscape had become more rugged and wild the closer they were to Jackson's. She smiled as Bass approached, two takeout cups in his hands. He looked at home here, surrounded by wilderness, the harsh, unforgiving landscape a perfect backdrop for his chiseled face and sculpted body. It was as if she could see the wolf just below the surface: restless, ready, and waiting for blood. He passed her one of the cups, looking at her with a wild edge in his eyes. She stared at her wolf in human skin, wondering what he was thinking and why his wolf shone in his dark eyes.

"What are you thinking, Katalina?" he asked.

Katalina turned, walking toward the picnic benches positioned along the edge of the forest. She sat before answering. "I can see the wolf in your eyes. Are you worried?"

With great effort, Bass reined his wolf back. "Sorry. I'm a little on edge, but not worried."

"It's fine, Bass. Don't apologize for who you are." She grasped for a different subject. "So . . . Nico?"

He smiled fondly. "I think you'll like Nico. He's very . . . how to put it . . . real world."

"I noticed. How could the two of you possibly have grown up together? I'd have thought he was human in any other situation," she laughed.

"He joined the pack when I was ten. He was eight. His dad's a wolf, mother's human. She lives in the nearby town. She split from his dad before Nico was born. Apparently, his dad forgot to mention he was a shifter. Anyway, Nico stays with his dad most of the time, but visits his mom on weekends. Oh, and he goes to an ordinary school. He was never homeschooled like the rest of us."

"That explains it. He knows how we ordinary people live."

"Nothing about you, Katalina Winter, is ordinary," he said with a warm smile.

*No, I suppose not.*

The silence settled over them again, pressing down, suffocating.

Katalina sighed heavily. "Am I silly to still hope our problems will be solved without a fight?"

"Not silly, no, but in the world of shifters, there is a hierarchy. The alpha is law."

"But he's your father."

"Yes, and that is the only reason I've gotten away with so much. Nico says I'm a rebel, but I never saw it that way. I never disobeyed my father to enrage him. We just have very different views, and I refuse to do something I don't agree with. He's wanted your blood for nearly eighteen years. He's the alpha and there will be consequences for my disobedience."

She already knew the answer, but she had to ask him anyway. "Are you really willing to fight your father for me?"

"I am willing to do whatever it takes to keep you safe. You are my mate, Katalina. Without you, my life holds no meaning."

She reached across the table for his hand. "Let's go deal with my father first. Hopefully, he's going to be easier to convince than yours. Even though he's been nothing but an arrogant, stubborn ass since I met him."

"I believe we'll get through to Jackson."

"What makes you say that?" she asked.

"The way he looks at you, Katalina . . . he may have given you up, but he loves you. He's gone about everything the wrong way, but when it boils down to it, he just wants to have you in his life."

"He wanted me as a broodmare."

"You'll still give him pure babies. They'll just be mine." He flashed his cheeky smile.

"Getting a little ahead of yourself there, Sebastian."

"There is another thing, something I find quite interesting."

"And what would that be?"

"You're of River Run descent, yet your wolf doesn't answer to Jackson."

"What do you mean?"

"He's alpha. As alpha, he has the ability to control you. Only the very strong, dominant wolves can disobey a direct order. Jackson has tried to give you commands a number of times. I've felt the strength in the words, yet you've brushed them off."

"Sometimes it's as if his voice is pressing down on me, but then it passes. Why is that?"

"I'm not sure, really. You've only been able to change for a short while. You're dominant, yes, but not nearly as strong as you will be. Maybe it's simply because you've grown up away from the pack, so your wolf doesn't register them as family."

"All this wolf stuff hurts my head," she moaned, rubbing her temples.

"We will get through this, Kat, together."

Smiling, she got to her feet and pulled him toward herself. "Together," she breathed into his mouth as she stretched up on her tiptoes for a kiss.

# CHAPTER 23

The rest of the drive didn't take long at all. Before Katalina knew it, the scenery looked familiar, dark-green pine trees flanking either side of the narrow road.

She took a deep breath. "I've got a really bad feeling about this." She wrapped her arms around her middle. While her tummy did flips, her knee jiggled up and down, over and over in quick succession.

Bass glanced at her. "Are you all right?"

"I don't know. I feel kinda . . ." Her words choked in her mouth. They rounded the corner and discovered a great wall of fire blocking their path.

"Shit, we're too late," Bass muttered.

Katalina's head whipped around. "Too late? What do you mean? BASS!" Katalina's heart pounded in her ears, her knee jiggled faster, her fingers trembling. She wanted to scream, her mind on the edge of hysteria.

Bass didn't answer her as she shouted at him. Instead, he scanned the forest edge, his eyes focused and calculating. The truck swerved sharply, bouncing them into the woods. Arne barked beside her.

"Bass, what are you doing?" she screamed.

"Trying to find . . ."

"I don't understand. What is this?"

He didn't answer.

"Sebastian!" She felt the wolf in her rise to the surface, her growl coming through in Katalina's voice.

Bass slammed on the brakes, nearly sending Arne through the windshield. Bass turned to her, his face like stone, his eyes dark and hungry for blood.

"Dark Shadow has done this. They've trapped River Run in and they'll slaughter them all." His voice held the raspy edge of rage.

"What?" her voice was a haunted whisper, as she pictured all of the people she'd met. Toby, Cage, Karen . . . *They can't die.*

"Bass, Bass, they can't die. We can't let this happ-en." Her voice broke, the fear she felt overtaking her.

Bass turned and looked at her, his face fierce and determined. "Katalina, none of them will die. We're going to drive through, okay?"

She nodded silently, wiping the tears from her cheeks. Katalina held on to the seat, preparing for the drive, when she sensed someone. She met Bass's gaze; his look told her he'd sensed them, too.

She opened the door, looking for whoever approached.

"Katalina!" Bass hissed.

"It's okay. It's—" She never finished her sentence. Cage raced toward the truck a second later, his teeth bared and the hairs along his back standing on end. He slowed as he saw her but his eyes never left Bass.

Bass slowly and deliberately made his way toward Katalina, positioning himself in front of her.

Cage changed. "You think I'd harm her!" he growled. "Scum, all of you Dark Shadows."

"I'd be careful what you say if I were you!" Bass said in a low, hard tone.

"Or what?" Cage spat back.

"Oh, will you stop it!" Katalina stood between them, infuriated by their wolf-testosterone battle. "We don't have time for this. Cage, get in. We're driving through."

The forest around them was thick with smoke, the black plumes cutting off their air.

Bass started the truck as the smoke filtered through the vents. "Quick, Bass!" Katalina coughed.

He slammed his foot on the accelerator, causing the wheels to spin in the snow. They reached the wall of fire. One second they were surrounded by smoke, flames, and darkness; the next, all they could see was bright, glittering snow and the nightmare rolling out in slow motion before them. Blood and claws, screams and cries, and the victorious growls from the Dark Shadow wolves. There were too many Dark Shadow wolves for River Run to have any chance of winning. Katalina stared in disbelief and horror, her eyes wide with fear. Seeing Toby struggling under the weight of two wolves, Jackson slowly losing his battle, and more River Run wolves outnumbered and badly injured filled her with fury. The universe screamed death. The universe wanted blood.

Cage leapt from the still-moving truck, changing into his wolf midjump. He entered the fray without hesitation or fear as he raced across the snow, tearing down those in his path.

Katalina lurched forward as the truck slammed to a stop. Her head whipped to the side, Bass having already climbed out, his clothes dropping to the ground.

"Stay in the truck," he ordered, before disappearing.

Her eyes tracked him, her shadow wolf, beautiful even as he dealt out death.

She sat in the truck frozen, stunned, detached from the world. Her breath rasped in and out; her heart battered an unrelenting beat. She climbed out of the car, her hands trembling while the wolf within her stirred.

A scream caught her attention and she whipped around, her back pressed up against the truck; it was Karen's scream. Karen's eyes, huge and full of tears, stared at Toby, her arms held protectively around two small boys.

Toby was losing his battle. Katalina couldn't tear her eyes away. She watched in growing rage as he collapsed under the weight of three wolves.

"Toby!" Her scream tore from her, echoing around them.

The keening howls in reply broke her. Katalina's clothes floated to the ground as she ran, her wolf bursting from her skin.

As white as the snow and as deadly as the predator she was, Katalina met the Dark Shadow wolves with the full fury of her loss and her grief. Claws slashing and jaw snapping, she used the weight of her wolf to barrel into them, sending them tumbling away from Toby. Crouching low and snarling, she crept toward the wolves. Her hackles rose, every cell of her being craving blood.

The Dark Shadow wolves were a mixture of brown and black, their eyes cold and filled with hatred. The three of them fanned out around her. Standing her ground, Katalina positioned herself between them and the River Run wolves they wished to kill. The middle wolf stepped forward. He was twice the size of Katalina's wolf and didn't seem at all intimidated. He lunged forward, closing the distance between them. In a split second, Katalina twisted away, her light body nimble and quick. She felt the brush of his claws through her fur, the slight scrape across skin. She snarled angrily as she slammed herself into his side, snapping her jaw down into flesh.

He shook her off, sending her tumbling to the ground with a yelp. Katalina climbed back to her feet, feeling pain throughout her muscles. Bass's loud angry bark surrounded her. His presence filled her and she sensed his need to reach her. Her eyes stayed fixed on the three wolves before her. They crowded closer together, stepping forward, herding her back toward the house.

Blood pumping with tension, she recognized the inevitable point of no return; she took another step back as they jumped forward, and hit the wall of the house. An angry growl tore from her chest as she crouched low, hackles raised. She waited for them to make their move, waited for the impact and pain. Katalina watched the wolf in the center tense, his muscles bunched and flexed. Katalina turned her head away, braced for the moment he'd attack.

A flash of black followed by an echoing thud filled her keen senses.

Katalina's bark was one of surprise. He'd reached her. The other two wolves scattered away as Bass sunk his teeth into the throat of the wolf. A quick snap of his jaw and the wolf went slack, dropping dead to the ground. He turned to her, blood dripping from his mouth, the sharp gleam of his teeth a reminder of the deadly predator he was. He whimpered, pushing his muzzle against her side. He couldn't speak human words, but she understood exactly what he meant. *Are you okay?* She whimpered softly in return, licking at a gash down his flank.

A high-pitched whine startled them back to the present. Cage and Jackson were being herded toward them by Dark Shadow wolves. The wolf they were protecting was bleeding badly, the back leg he dragged hanging limp. The members of Jackson's pack were still outnumbered two to one, and the Dark Shadow wolves looked in far better condition than the remaining River Run wolves.

Frightened, Katalina pressed up against Bass's side. She wasn't prepared for the violence of this new world. He turned back to her with a reassuring lick.

He ran toward Jackson and Cage. Katalina followed. She might not have been trained to fight, or have grown up in this world, but she couldn't stand back and watch the people she cared for get hurt. The wolves clashed together, teeth tearing, claws ripping. The thud of bodies and whimpers of pain were brutal. Katalina fell back, her legs a tangle beneath her and her white fur stained with blood. Panting heavily, she forced herself to get back up. About to jump back into the chaos, Bass stepped forward. The snarl that ripped from him radiated rage, and the power in his voice halted the Dark Shadow wolves.

Everyone—both Dark Shadow and River Run—paused and stared. It was as if the world held its breath: the wind halted, the flames froze, not a single sound could be heard.

Katalina watched, stunned and in awe, as Bass changed, his skin stained with blood and the long wisps of his hair plastered to his neck with sweat.

"I am your alpha's son and I order you to stop this!" his voice boomed into the quiet.

The Dark Shadow wolves snarled back in protest.

"ENOUGH!"

Even though his words weren't directed at her, Katalina could still feel the effect of his voice, the shiver over her skin, the pressure to obey.

"Go back to my father and tell him no more River Run blood will be shed." The wolves crouched down low to the ground, their eyes hard and their heads shaking as if to clear his voice from their minds.

"I said GO!" He took a step forward, his human words disappearing into a growl.

They started to back away but one remained. He took a step forward, snarling.

"You challenge me?" Bass asked.

The wolf changed into a man. "Your father is my alpha. I take orders from him only." He leapt, his body contorting, changing into a wolf.

The next moment happened so fast, Katalina's startled yelp was still vibrating through the air as the Dark Shadow wolf landed dead at Bass's feet. She stared at his right paw, coated red with blood, marking the white snow.

The moment their fellow wolf fell dead, Dark Shadow scattered.

Katalina felt the change ripple through her body and ran forward on two feet, reaching him as Bass's knees buckled from under him.

"Bass!" she gasped, her hands reaching for him.

"I'm fine. I'm fine," he murmured as she held him in her arms, her eyes scanning every inch of him for a mortal wound. "Using that much strength took it out of me, that's all."

"I don't understand. What just happened? How did you do that?"

His eyes met hers. "Another time, Katalina. We are still in danger."

Katalina's head turned to see the angry glint of wolf eyes watching them. Jackson changed, his tall, broad frame towering over them.

"Katalina, step away from him!"

"No!" she shouted back. "He's just saved all of you, yet you still can't see through your hatred!" She positioned herself in front of Bass, staring Jackson in the eyes, showing him how fierce and resolute she was, showing him she wouldn't back down.

"Kat!" Bass hissed, dragging her behind him.

"You haven't got time for this, Jackson!" Karen's stern voice forced Jackson to look away. "Take a look at your people, Jackson. Are you pleased with what you've accomplished?"

Karen bent over Toby, her hands quickly and gently assessing him. "Cage, quickly now! Bring him inside." Karen said one last thing before the door shut behind her: "I need help, Jackson, if you'd like no more of your pack to die."

Jackson didn't move, but he bellowed orders from where he stood. "Cage! Call your fath—"

Cage appeared in the doorway, phone to his ear. "I'm already on it! He says they've nearly put out the fire behind us. It doesn't seem to be spreading because of the snow. He has every available pack member he could get hold of."

"Good. Help Karen. William, drag your ass inside and have that leg seen to."

He turned his attention back to Katalina. "Katalina, you're not going anywhere."

Katalina straightened back up and pulled the sweater she'd picked up over her head. Bass returned to her seconds later, his jeans hung low on his hips.

"I will do as I please. But if you wish to talk, I'll listen."

He opened his mouth as if to speak.

"First you can put on some clothes! In your world, it may be just fine to talk to your daughter naked, but in my world, they'd lock you up." She put her hands on her hips and glared.

"Fine!" Jackson huffed. He turned on his heel and stomped into the house.

Katalina laughed. "I swear, sometimes he acts like a child."

"Katalina, it may be in our favor if you could not wind him up further," Bass scolded with a smile. "Here, I found your jeans. They're a little wet but . . ."

Katalina took the jeans, pulling them on, and then stretched up on her toes, kissing him silently. "I ever tell you how much I love you?"

His hands gripped her hips, scorching her bare skin. "Possibly, but maybe you should demonstrate how much later?" His voice was like gravel grazing over her skin, making her tummy flutter with anticipation.

This is what Katalina loved most about Bass. No matter the situation, no matter the danger they were in, it took only one touch for them to be in their own world, for nothing to matter but their hushed, secret whispers, heated stares, and consuming love.

"Kat!" It was Jackson, who had reemerged from the house fully clothed.

Katalina sighed, breaking away from Bass. She took hold of his hand and walked toward Jackson. "Time to face the music," she muttered.

"Play nice," Bass whispered into her ear, "and I'll reward you later."

# CHAPTER 24

They walked toward Jackson, hands linked together. Katalina could see the tension in every fiber of Jackson's body—from the rigid set of his jaw to his knuckles strained against white skin. She pressed herself closer to Bass, trying to gain control of the anxiety churning inside of her.

As if sensing her feelings, Bass squeezed her hand. "I'm right here," he whispered.

Katalina took her eyes off Jackson for just the barest of seconds. She lifted the corner of her mouth slightly, squeezing Bass's hand back. Her eyes met his, the tension dropping from her face, but then Jackson wrenched Katalina away from Bass. The space between them was like a tear within her soul.

The wolf within her rose up and drove Katalina to react. She pulled back from Jackson's grip, and her free hand swung up, palm open, and slapped him across the face. The noise from the impact vibrated through the air. Jackson stood speechless, his hand slowly pressing against the red patch that had formed on the side of his face.

"Never touch me again!" Any anxiety she'd felt before had vanished. Now Katalina was the one who stood rigid with tension, her blood hot with anger. "I don't care who you are; no one has the right to touch me in that way."

Bass's arm reached out and pulled her gently backward. She went willingly into his warm embrace.

Their actions seemed to snap Jackson from his shock, his angry mask slipping once more into place.

"This cannot happen," he ground out through clenched teeth, his finger pointing at both of them. "He is Dark Shadow, Katalina. I forbid this!"

"Forbid it! Forbid it!" Katalina growled in frustration, stepping forward, her angry gaze fixed on Jackson. "Have you heard yourself? You can't forbid me to do anything. I will love whom I wish. I will do exactly what I WISH!" Her voice rose the more she talked. Her blood was on fire; any minute she was going to combust.

"Katalina, will you just stop and think about this for a minute? He's Dark Shadow, you are River Run. Whether you want to be or not, that is who you are. My blood runs through your veins."

Katalina sucked in an angry breath and blew it out as she looked at the ground. "I honestly can't see why that is a problem. It shouldn't matter who I'm with as long as he loves me. You say you're my father, but you act nothing like one. All that should matter to you is that I'm happy and that I'm loved. I know that's what my dad would want for me." She looked up to see indecision cloud Jackson's eyes.

He ran his hands angrily through his long, messy red hair, then pressed them tightly over his eyes. His voice was low and defeated. "It was never supposed to be this way."

"Maybe you're right, Jackson. Maybe I was supposed to be with Cage. Maybe I was supposed to grow up with my pack, my biological family. Cage and I would have been best friends and teenage sweethearts. Maybe we would have married, and had those precious, pureblooded babies you so desperately want. Maybe that is how my life should have been, but it didn't turned out that way, did it?"

Katalina let out a long breath before continuing. "You gave me away before I was even one. Dumped me on a doorstep. I didn't grow up with a pack. I grew up with normal parents, in a normal home. I wasn't a shifter. I was just an ordinary human girl. But then you changed your mind, and that decision cost me my parents, the life I knew. You've dragged me into this brutal world, a world that makes no sense to me, one full of blood and death, where it's perfectly okay to attack one another." Glancing away, she stared at the horizon, focusing on nothing. "I feel lost here, Jackson. Every decision you've made for me since I turned eighteen has cut me. My heart bleeds because of you and decisions you have made. I have lost everything I've ever known and you don't seem to give a shit. And now you want to take away the only person I have left, the one thing that makes sense in this life. Well, guess what, Jackson? I honestly couldn't give a damn what you want. I hate you for everything you've done to me. Do you understand that?"

Breathing heavily, feeling too angry to cry or move, she stared at the angry, bitter man with whom she shared DNA and wondered what parts of him she'd inherited.

The silence between them was a palpable thing. Thick and heavy, it seemed to choke the air from their lungs until finally Jackson spoke. His green eyes looked up but connected with Bass, not Katalina.

"She says she loves you, but do you love her?"

"She's my mate," Bass replied, matter-of-factly.

Jackson nodded. "I'm trying to work out what you're planning. Do you want River Run or do you simply wish to destroy me by taking the last link I have to my Winter?"

Bass frowned as he thought over Jackson's words. He didn't seem offended by what he'd said, but Katalina sure was.

"How dare you! Can't he just love me for me? Not everything is about your freaking pack!"

"Katalina, it's fine." Bass ran his hand gently across her face. "Jackson has every right to know my intentions. After all, I did go into that shed to kill you."

Jackson's growl cut Bass short.

Katalina saw the slightest smile cross Bass's lips before his neutral expression returned. She finally understood what Nico meant when he said Bass could talk himself out of arguments. Jackson looked physically pained as he tried to control his anger. He looked as if he'd love nothing more than to punch Bass, but while Bass was so calm, he could do nothing but try to restrain himself.

"What? Isn't that what you wanted to hear? Did you think I sought her out with the intention of stealing her away? That I wanted to take your pack? Well, I'm sorry to inform you, I never intended to take River Run—I intended to fulfill my father's wishes. You see, he thought it would be quite poetic if his son killed your daughter. He's trained me from the moment I could walk so that I would be ready, but then I saw her. Beautiful and broken, dressed in white, with the moonlight in her hair, she looked like an angel, an angel stained red with blood. I knew who she was to me the moment I saw her. I didn't think about the consequences. She's mine and that is all that matters.

"You should understand what I mean when I say she's my mate. Those lucky enough to find the one person on this planet who is made for them will stop at nothing to keep them safe, and if they fail . . . Well, this war is proof of the pain the one left behind feels. She is my mate, Jackson. That is all the explanation you should need."

Jackson stared. Bass stared back. Neither seemed like he was going to back down.

Katalina threw her hands up. She'd had enough; she was too tired to fight, too heartbroken to care anymore. All she wanted to do was get as far away from Jackson as possible and forget he had ever existed. "I'm leaving. Tell Toby I'm sorry I couldn't stay."

She turned on the spot, her hair fanning around her. The late evening sun made each fine thread glisten as she strode away. She didn't wait to see if Bass followed; she wasn't even sure she wanted him to follow.

*I intended to fulfill my father's wishes . . .*

"Ugh, stupid asshole," she muttered. Sometimes she forgot he was a shifter. He'd been so different in her world, relaxed and funny, but in this world, in his world—*her new world*—he was an alpha's son: controlled, practical, acting with logic and not emotion.

*How could he talk so flippantly about going against his father?*

"Katalina, where are you going?" Bass ran past her. He walked backward in front of her as she stomped. "Kat?"

"I'm leaving. I don't care where. Anywhere that isn't here." She'd reached the truck. Opening the door, she let Arne out.

"What's the matter? Didn't you hear what he said? He's accepting us, Kat."

Katalina stopped. "I don't need his acceptance, Bass," she sighed. "I didn't come here for approval."

"Why did you come here then?" he asked gently.

"I'm not even sure I know. I'm not sure of anything anymore. It's all messed up. Everything is a mess. I'm a mess."

"No, you're not."

"Yes I am. How can you not see that?"

He tried to take her hand but she pulled away. "Don't. Just leave me, Bass."

"I can't do that, Kat."

She looked at him, at the boy who could be two people, who could change from *her* Bass to Sebastian Evernight in the blink of an eye. When she looked at him now, there was no doubt of his love, but she just couldn't shake his words, the way he spoke so unemotionally to Jackson.

"I can feel you're mad at me but I don't understand why," he said.

"Argh!" she screamed. She shoved him, her hands taking on a life of their own.

"Do you know what I don't understand? I don't understand how you can talk about wanting to kill me in such an offhand tone. It is not *nothing*, Sebastian!"

"Don't call me that."

"Why? It's who you are being."

"Kat, you are being irrational."

"Irrational! I'm fucking livid!" It infuriated her that he could stay so calm when she felt ready to rip him apart. She knew she wasn't really that mad at him. She was just angry in general: angry at the world, at Jackson, at herself.

They stood there, Bass calm, the frown mark between his eyes the only outward sign of emotion, and Katalina furious, her hands in fists.

"I don't know what you want me to do," he said quietly.

Katalina looked at him as he sighed. She breathed deeply, then released her breath, uncurling each finger as she did. Her anger dissolved in a puff of breath. "Get mad, Bass. Shout, scream, do something other than act as if nothing affects you."

"Is that what you think? That none of this affects me? That the thought of laying a single finger on my father doesn't tear me up inside? Do you think I don't hate myself every minute of every day for ever thinking of hurting you? Because I do, Kat. I feel as lost and as angry at what we've been dealt as you. The difference is, I've had years to perfect my mask, to play the game, to be Sebastian Evernight."

"I'm not sure I like this mask."

She went into his arms as he reached for her this time. "Sometimes the mask comes in handy." His hands cradled her face, so gently it nearly broke her. "Only three people know the real me and one of them is dead."

"Nico and your grandmother?" she asked.

He nodded. "And you."

"I don't want to be responsible for you having to do such horrible things."

"Kat, whatever happens next will not be on you. What happens between me and my father will be on him. You must stop thinking of him as my dad. He isn't. He's been nothing more than my alpha, and not a nice one at that. He has never shown me any love. He stole my childhood by forcing me to fight. He's pushed me and pushed me, and nothing I have ever done has been good enough. I stopped trying to please him a very long time ago, and I stopped seeing him as my father way before that."

"I'm sorry," she whispered.

"Don't be." He kissed her cheek. "Are you ready to go back?" He turned her around in his arms. "It looks like a few more people have arrived."

"Oh goody!"

Bass smiled against her neck, nipping at her skin. "I do love you, my snarky girl."

They walked back toward the house, a hive of activity.

"I'm still not sure I fit in this world."

"It doesn't matter. We'll make the world fit you."

# CHAPTER 25

The house was in chaos when they walked in. Katalina stopped in the doorway, stunned. There was a trail of bloodstained rags leading to the kitchen; she could hear Jackson from the front room, his voice raised.

"Come on." Katalina pulled on Bass's hand, leading him toward the kitchen. She wasn't in the mood to face Jackson. One step into the kitchen proved she wasn't ready for this either. Toby lay on the kitchen table. He was deathly pale and unmoving. Karen worked over him, her hands quick and sure in their task. A woman—Katalina assumed she was Toby's mother—stood nearby, hovering but looking as if she didn't dare approach. Tears of black mascara streamed down her face.

"Is h-he g-going to be okay?" Katalina stammered.

Karen didn't look up, but she answered, "He'd have been dead if not for you, Kat. Toby is a strong boy. He'll fight."

Karen's answer caused Toby's mother to choke out a sob. She buried her face in her hands. "Terry, why don't you go find Cage? I'll come get you when Toby wakes up."

Katalina watched in silence as Terry nodded and left the kitchen.

"Kat, come here and help me."

"What? No, I'd be no use." She suddenly wished she'd chosen Jackson. Jackson shouting was far easier to handle than Toby bleeding to death.

"Hold this!" Karen ordered.

Katalina walked forward on numb legs. She took the flashlight from Karen. "I need you to shine the light in here. There's a bleed I need to find."

Katalina wasn't sure how long she stood there, holding a flashlight over Toby's open body. She focused on forcing her breaths in and out, deep and steady, over and over. She didn't know how Karen did it, how she had her hands inside someone, surrounded by organs and blood.

"Gotcha," Karen muttered. "Pass me that clamp, Kat."

"Clamp?" Katalina whispered, looking at the tray of instruments next to her. Her hand hovered over what she thought looked like a clamp.

"That's the one." With an unsteady hand, Katalina handed it over and Karen carried on.

Once Karen had stitched Toby up and put a dressing over the wound, Katalina turned around to look for Bass, but he'd gone.

"Kat, tell Terry she can come back, please," Karen called as Katalina left to find Bass.

She found him near the front door, gazing out the window. He turned with a smile at her approach. Katalina paused at the open door to the front room. Terry sat in the corner chair, staring into space but no longer crying.

"You can go see him now, Terry," Katalina said.

Terry's faraway eyes fixed on her. She stared for a second before her brain registered Katalina's words. "Thank you," she murmured, jumping to her feet.

As she walked toward Bass, Katalina heard Jackson having a heated discussion with a woman who looked to be in her late thirties. She held the hands of twin boys. They didn't seem the least bit affected by the madness of the last few hours, but their mother clearly was.

Katalina had almost made it to Bass when her name fell from Jackson's lips. She froze, a deer in headlights, wondering whether it would be rude if she turned and ran.

"Kat, have you met Amelia and her two boys, Thomas and George?"

"N-no," Katalina stammered, still in the hallway. She shifted from one foot to the other, contemplating escape.

"Come say hello. Amelia, this is my daughter, Katalina. You see, I have my child here where it's safe."

*Great, he's using me to put across his point!*

Katalina sighed, having no choice but to say hello to Amelia. "Hi, it's nice to meet you."

Amelia gazed at Katalina, her mouth set in a hard line. "Hello, Katalina. I'm pleased you are back home, but your father is trying to distract me."

Katalina smiled. "I gathered that, and it's just *Jackson*. My father died a few weeks ago."

"Oh, um, I-I'm sorry," Amelia stammered.

Katalina smiled sadly but said nothing. Jackson's eyes darted between them agitatedly, his plan clearly not working.

"Hey, Thomas, George, do you want to come with me and see my dog, while your mommy and Jackson talk?" Katalina crouched down as she asked them.

"Sure!" they both chimed in unison, ripping their hands from their mother's grip.

Amelia look startled. She clearly didn't want to let them go, but she didn't have a valid excuse to say so. "Boys, we're leaving, so you can't today."

"Aww!" they moaned.

"Amelia, please, you're safest here. At least wait until I can have someone go with you," Jackson pleaded.

"This place was attacked just a short while ago. I'm taking my chances at home. I'm sure they wouldn't attack a mother and her children anyway. It's you they want. As far as I'm concerned, the farther aw—"

Bass's voice cut through the room, halting her conversation. "They would."

"I beg your pardon?"

"Dark Shadow would attack a mother and her children."

Amelia gasped, clutching her chest. "A-and who are you?"

"Sebastian Evernight."

"Evernight? Is-isn't that a Dark Shadow name?" she asked in a small voice.

"Yes."

"Oh my God!" Amelia gasped, reaching for her boys' hands again. She turned her angry gaze on Jackson. "You want me to stay here with him? Nowhere is safe anymore."

"He's not going to hurt anyone," Katalina said firmly, cutting Amelia's ranting short.

"And how would you know that?" Amelia had gone from concerned to outraged. She glared at Katalina.

"Hey now, don't you talk to her like that," Jackson cut in.

"That's all right, Jackson. I can take care of myself." Katalina took a step forward. "Because I know him. I know he'd never hurt anyone unless provoked, and because he's just defended all of you, against his own pack. He's killed to protect River Run. And because he's my mate." Katalina glared back at Amelia, her eyes unblinking. "Now listen to Jackson and stop acting irrationally. It doesn't make sense for you to take off with two children, unprotected, when it's clear some of Dark Shadow would like us all dead."

Amelia stared, dumbstruck. Her boys snickered.

Katalina turned and strode out of the room. She took Bass's hand as she left, dragging him out into the hallway and closing the door behind them to muffle Amelia's renewed ranting.

Katalina dropped with a huff on to the stairs, using the steps as a seat. "Is it too late to change my mind and hide at my grandmother's forever?" she asked the floor.

Bass just laughed. Arne stuck his head on her lap. She scratched behind his ears, trying to block out Jackson, who was sounding more irritated by the second.

"I just made that worse, right?" she asked Bass, looking up to find him standing by the front door, his fingers playing with the net curtain hanging over the small window.

"You were doing okay until you mentioned your mate's a Dark Shadow."

"But my mate is a Dark Shadow and they are just going to have to deal with it."

He glanced at her with a smile just as Amelia pulled open the front-room door. Her twin boys followed, seemingly enjoying the drama. "We are leaving!" she shouted, grabbing the boys' coats and throwing them at Thomas and George.

"No, you are not!" Jackson boomed back.

"What's going on?" Karen asked as she rushed in from the kitchen. It was utter chaos, shouting, staring. The back door banged open as Cage ran in. He froze for a second as he took in the scene, and then decided what he had to say was more important.

"Bodies are all collected and covered in the back of the truck." His voiced carried over the ranting and raving.

Katalina buried her head in her hands, wanting to disappear.

"Someone's here," Bass said into the noise.

Jackson spun around, turning his back on Amelia just as the door opened. More people crowded into the already-packed hallway. Amelia pushed past Jackson, racing for the door, her knuckles strained white as she gripped her little boys' hands.

"No, you don't!" Jackson moved with such speed, Katalina couldn't follow the movement. One minute Amelia was making a run for it, the next Jackson was lifting her from the floor, his thick muscular arm wrapped around her middle.

The three men who had walked in looked on in surprise. Katalina decided this was the craziest family reunion ever.

"I didn't want to do this but you leave me no choice." Jackson sighed before he spoke his next words. His tone changed. The power and strength in his words was palpable in the air, the command an unbreakable thing. "As your alpha, I forbid you to leave this house unless given permission by me."

Jackson put her down, dismissing her. "What do you know?" he asked the men standing with their backs against the closed door.

The eldest of the three was about to answer, but Bass interrupted. "Jackson." Everyone went silent, staring at him as if they couldn't believe he'd spoken.

"Yes?" Jackson half growled.

"We've got company: cops."

"Shit!" Jackson ran his hands through his hair with a groan. "Everyone in the back, now! Not a word out of any of you."

Katalina jumped to her feet. "Come on, boy," she murmured, patting her leg as she instructed Arne to follow.

People scrambled into action, pushing their way through the door into the kitchen.

Katalina heard Karen speak in a firm tone. "Everyone over there. I don't want Toby disturbed."

"Look at this place! It's like a war zone!" Jackson shouted, looking at the bloodied rags strewn across the floor.

Katalina picked them up as she walked.

"William, what the fuck are you doing, sitting bleeding on my floor? I told you to go see Karen."

Katalina came back into the hall to see what was taking Bass so long.

"Well, someone had to keep an eye on him. Dark Shadow scum!" William spat.

Bass froze in his path. Katalina saw the hurt cross his face for the briefest of moments before his mask slipped back into place.

"And how exactly did you plan to stop him with a broken leg? Cage, come get this idiot off my floor!"

Cage appeared through the doorway, took one look at William, and laughed, "Come on, buddy."

There was a knock at the door.

Jackson's eyes looked at the pool of blood William had left behind.

The knock came again, louder.

Katalina pulled a towel from off the banister and rushed forward to mop the blood up. "Get the door," she hissed.

"Just a second," Jackson called toward the door. "Both of you stay out of sight. I don't want either one of you caught up in this."

They slipped into the kitchen in silence. William lay on the floor with Cage at his shoulders holding him down. Karen's fingers prodded at his leg, causing William to moan in pain.

"Shush. Jackson's talking to the cops," Katalina hissed.

Karen looked up at her. "Kat, come help."

Katalina tossed the towel aside and dropped on her knees beside Karen.

"What do you need?"

"Well, the stupid idiot didn't come to me straight away, so his leg's healing crooked. I'm going to have to rebreak it. I want you to hold his thigh down. Cage, hold his shoulders. Here, William, bite on this. No noise, remember."

Katalina watched as Karen knelt at his feet. She took his foot in her hands and pulled. The crack echoed through the silence. William's muffled cry sent a shiver down Katalina's spine.

Jackson popped in briefly to inform them of the cops' departure and then disappeared to do something else. Hoping to escape now that the cops had left and William's leg had been straightened, Katalina started to stand, but Karen gave her more instructions and before she knew it, she was lost in the task at hand.

Katalina followed Karen's directions, not thinking of anything else. It was a shock a little while later when she felt the first trickle of anxiety form in her gut. She focused on the feeling, wondering where it had come from, because although treating injured people wasn't the most pleasant task, it was nice to feel needed, to help. It took her a minute to realize it wasn't her own feeling she was experiencing, but Bass's. She glanced up from holding the splint while Karen strapped William's leg in place. Bass stood alone in the corner, his eyes glazed, staring at nothing. To anyone else in the room, he looked as indifferent as he always did, but to Katalina he looked lost, and Bass never looked lost. He was the type of person who owned a room. As if he sensed her looking, his glazed eyes focused on her. He flashed a forced smile.

"Hey, Karen, can I leave you to it? There's something I have to do."

Karen glanced up at Katalina and then to Bass. "Sure, Kat, thanks for your help."

Walking silently to him, Katalina took Bass's hand and led him out the back door. Arne stood from his position by the twins, but Katalina told him to stay. Once outside, she turned to face Bass and squeezed his hand as she asked, "Are you all right?"

"Of course. Why wouldn't I be?"

"Bass, I'm not stupid. I can read you better than you think. What's wrong?"

"I'm fine." He sounded pained.

Katalina took his hand and placed it over her heart. "I know I'm not as good at this shifter stuff as you, but I know this feeling inside of me is yours, and not mine. Talk to me. You're anxious, fearful even."

Bass sighed, "It's hard to explain."

"Try." She gave him an encouraging smile.

"These people, River Run, they love you. You might not have grown up in the pack, but to them, you've always been a member. I can see it, how easily you fit in."

"I'm not so sure I fit in, but isn't them accepting me a good thing?"

"Yes. It's just . . . they look at me and see Dark Shadow. These are your people, but they may never accept me. I don't want you to resent me—or them—because I don't fit in your world."

"Sebastian Evernight, you are my world." Standing on tiptoes, she placed a soft kiss on his lips. "Please don't feel like that. Give them time. I belong here about as much as you do. I've never been in a pack and I certainly won't be taking orders from Jackson. We'll just take each day as it comes, but I promise you, I'd never want to be anywhere other than by your side."

# CHAPTER 26

They didn't go back inside. Bass stood behind Katalina with his arms wrapped around her. She melted into his hold, her body molding against the hard planes of his torso. "Right here, this is my home," she whispered to him, tipping her head to the side and kissing him along his jaw. The few-days-old stubble rubbed against her sensitive skin.

"How are you coping, Kat? Having to fight—I know it's not something you wanted to do."

Katalina stood in his embrace, watching as the sun slid its way down the sky. She could see the distant outlines of people still working to put out the fire. The sun lit the smoke, turning the plumes into a canvas of purples and oranges. She thought about driving through the fire and the feeling of being transported into another world. She remembered every beat of her heart as she watched Toby fall and not get back up. She recalled the anger and driving need inside of her, to protect, to stop those wanting to hurt the people she cared for.

"I honestly feel fine. I've come to realize something: fighting and protecting others is in my blood. My wolf could never stand back and watch others fight for her, and she's as much a part of me as my human half. I suppose I feared that if I accepted who I am, then I would lose my old self. I wouldn't be Katalina Winter anymore. My wolf has always been a part of me. I was born shifter, not human, and I've been denying my true self long enough."

Katalina felt Bass's lips against her neck, his breath hot against her skin. He breathed in, opening his mouth to speak, but the back door opened, cutting him off. They both looked up to see who'd come outside.

"Jackson," Bass murmured with a nod.

"What did you say to the police?" Katalina asked.

"I didn't have much to tell them other than someone decided to set fire to my land. They didn't buy it but they can't prove otherwise. They're gone for now." Jackson's eyes narrowed at the sight of Bass's arms wrapped around Katalina. He looked to be having an argument with himself. He took a deep breath and with a hand on his neck, he said, "Kat, we need to talk."

*I can't wait.*

Bass stepped back from Katalina, but his hand remained tight around hers.

"Both of you, really," Jackson stated, looking more uncomfortable by the minute.

"We're listening," Katalina muttered, glaring.

"Right, well, I'm not going to say I'm happy about this, but I understand I have no right to dictate your life, and even if I did, there is little I can do to stop a mating. It's very clear you're mates. I only need to watch the two of you to see that. The way you move and act together, it's as if you've known each other for years. I sincerely wish it had been Cage, not because I don't like Sebastian—and honestly, Kat, he's strong, stronger than Cage, and he's obviously willing to protect you—but he's Dark Shadow, Kat. His father is their alpha, and quite frankly, I'm losing this war. I'm not sure I can protect you. I'm worried,

Kat. I made a mistake giving you away, and now I'm frightened I'm going to lose you again."

Stunned, Katalina had no idea what to say. This was the first real conversation she'd had with him. The first time she actually felt as if she was listening to her father.

Bass saved her from having to speak. "It's my job to protect Katalina. I will deal with my father."

"Okay, so you have a plan?" Jackson asked.

"Yes, I'm going to talk to my father. See if I can reason with him."

Katalina thought Jackson's eyes might bulge out of his head. He linked his hands behind his neck, staring at Bass as if he'd gone mad. Bass had his mask in place, looking cool and collected, as if nothing fazed him.

"Talk? And you think he'll listen?"

"Not at all. I think he'll see my mating to Katalina as the ultimate betrayal and finally have an excuse to kill me."

Jackson actually laughed. He turned toward the house and then back around. "Wonderful," he muttered. "Well, correct me if I'm wrong, but your plan sucks."

Katalina tugged the hand she held. "Bass, I'm sure your father will listen. Look at Jackson. He's come around."

Bass looked her straight in the eyes. "My father is nothing like Jackson. He will want to kill me—but I'm going to kill him."

"Bass!" Katalina gasped.

"What are you? Like, twenty?" Jackson asked.

"Nineteen."

"Right, nineteen and you've got the strength to take on an alpha and lead a pack like Dark Shadow?"

"I never said it was an easy plan, but there are a lot of members in Dark Shadow who follow my father through fear, not loyalty."

"Shit! This is the craziest half-assed plan I've ever heard."

"When I lead Dark Shadow, Katalina will be safe and so will you."

"I'm not denying that, but let me ask you something, Sebastian. Are you ready to kill your own father? Mentally and physically?"

"He's not killing anyone! This is crazy. I can't listen to this. How can the two of you stand there talking so casually about killing someone? Your own freaking dad, Bass." Katalina stormed off, ripping her hand from Bass's. She slammed the door as she stomped in, rattling the side of the house.

"Kat!" Bass called after her.

"Leave her," Jackson said, taking hold of his arm. "You need to answer me, boy. You truly want me to accept you. I need to hear you say it."

Bass pulled out of Jackson's hold and faced him head-on. He let the wolf inside of him rise to the surface, allowed his true self to come forward.

"I have been preparing for this day all my life. I have never gotten along with him, and I have always seen the world differently than him. I always knew there'd be a day when he'd push me too far, when I couldn't stand by and watch his cruelty anymore. And as for my physical strength, I'm not sure. I thought I'd have more time, but my time's up. I don't have a choice anymore."

"Does he know how strong you are?"

"I'm not stupid, Jackson. I've always stayed under the radar. I've never fought for dominance or a higher ranking within the pack. But neither is my father stupid. He's had me training from the moment I could walk, always pushed me so I could defend myself against River Run, but I don't think he knows the full extent of my power; otherwise, I'd have been dead a long time ago."

The back door swung open. Cage's head popped out. "Everything all right? Kat's trying to knock the house down."

"Yeah," Jackson answered. "Has the fire crew left yet?"

"Dad's just gone out to see them off. What are we doing with them?" Cage nodded toward the truck with the dead Dark Shadows in the back.

"Return them," Bass interrupted.

Cage took a step forward, his hands in fists. The door shut with a click behind him. "What makes you think you have a say in this?" he ground out.

"All right, Cage, I haven't got the energy for this," Jackson said, taking a step, positioning himself in front of Bass, and blocking Cage's view.

This only enraged Cage more. "So it's like that now, is it? You trust him enough to put your back to him!"

"Two of those men died by his hands, Cage. If he'd wanted me dead, all he'd have needed to do was stand by and watch."

Cage glared for a moment longer before storming into the house. The walls rattled behind him.

"Gonna need a new house at this rate," Jackson muttered. Turning to Bass, he said, "Why should I return them? They came here to kill me."

"It's not their fault. All they did was follow orders. Disobeying my father is a death sentence. There are no second chances. You follow or you die. Two of those men have mates and children. Let them bury their loved ones on pack land."

"Fair enough, but you can return them. Keys are in the truck."

Bass nodded. He walked to the truck; halfway there he turned to speak. "Tell Kat I won't be long."

"I'll have Karen check on her. Think she'd like to hit me again. That girl sure has a temper."

The door closed. Bass started the engine, smiling to himself as he imagined Katalina punching Jackson.

# CHAPTER 27

Katalina stood at the window, watching Bass drive away. In a way, she'd come full circle. Once again she was staring at the endless snow-dusted treetops. Only this time, she wasn't contemplating escape; rather, she was considering how to stay without anyone else dying.

There was a soft knock at her door. "You can come in, Karen," Katalina said, not moving her eyes from the view outside.

"Starting to use your wolf senses," Karen said.

"Where's he going?" she asked, ignoring Karen's observation.

"He's taking the dead back home. He said he wouldn't be long."

Kat crossed her arms, needing a shield from the world.

"Kat, are you okay?" Karen asked softly.

Katalina let out a long, sad breath before facing Karen. "No, I'm not."

"The attack a bit too much for you?"

"Honestly, Karen, I'm not sure how I feel. I'm numb. Defending Toby was as easy as breathing. There was no thought, just instinct. I just . . . all this death. I watch all of you, so immune to it all; you just accept it as life."

"I'm afraid it is, Kat."

"Well, it's not where I come from. He's going against his dad for me. He's willing to do anything. How can I even look him in the eye? He's willing to give up so much . . . to do so much. How do we have a calm conversation about that?"

"Oh, Kat, he loves you. You're his mate, and he won't . . . he can't stop until you are safe."

"Surely there's another way?" Katalina asked, feeling hopeless.

"In our world, the alpha is law. To challenge his word is to challenge his position. A pack only gets a new alpha if the old one steps down or dies. Maybe he'll surprise Sebastian and accept you as Jackson has."

"Maybe," she answered, not sounding sure at all.

"Don't punish him for doing what is necessary."

"I'm not. I know this isn't his fault, but I wouldn't be me if I just accepted everything that's involved in a shifter's life. I'm more than a shifter, Karen. I need to hold on to the part of me that was raised by humans. If I lose myself, then they will truly be gone." She took a breath before carrying on. "Jackson and Winter gave me life, but my parents raised me. My beliefs were shaped by them."

"I understand, Kat." Karen was silent for a beat. "Toby's coming around. I'm sure he'll be pleased to see you."

"Okay, I'll be down in a minute."

Karen said one last thing before leaving Katalina alone. Her voice was the softest of whispers, and filled with the pride of a grandmother. "You're doing well, Kat. Don't change. Our world needs to see its mistakes."

Katalina let her go, answering silently: *Why do I have to be the one to change this world?*

*****

Propped up on a pillow, Toby drank from a straw in a cup his mother held for him. Cage hovered in the corner, staring at nothing but looking as if he had a lot on his mind. Katalina smiled at him as his eyes fixed on her for a second, but he didn't return it. He pushed off from the wall and started to leave.

"I'll run a perimeter check," he muttered as he left.

Katalina stared after him, wondering whether she should follow him, when Toby gasped her name. She looked at him with a smile, pleased to see his infectious, carefree personality still intact.

"Hey, you."

His mother stood up. "I'll go make you something to eat, Toby." She ruffled his hair before leaving.

"Mom! I'm not a baby," Toby whined.

"You're my baby!" she huffed.

Katalina laughed, sitting on the end of the sofa. "How do you feel?"

"Hurt like hell, but I'll be fine. Thanks to you."

"I didn't do much except give them somebody else to chomp on. Bass saved you."

"No, Kat, I'm alive because of you."

Katalina played with her hands in her lap, feeling a little uncomfortable; she wasn't ready to think about what she'd done.

"You were pretty badass, Kat," he laughed. "Ow! Best not do that."

Katalina sank into the sofa and put Toby's feet in her lap. She smiled. "Yep, that's me. I'm a real badass now, Toby. I have wolf senses and everything!" she joked.

"Yeah, and a mate! Gone for a week and you come back hitched."

"Hitched! I did not get married, Toby. Only old people get married."

"Pfft! Look pretty old to me!"

"If you weren't injured, I'd kick your butt with my new badass skills!"

Toby shook his head, trying not to laugh. "Dark Shadow, though! I can't believe you've mated a Dark Shadow wolf."

"Don't forget he's the alpha's son. That's the best part. I bet Jackson's wishing he'd left me where I was."

"I'm not. It's about time something interesting happened around here. This place was dull without you."

"Thanks, Toby. I'm pleased to be back."

"You mean that or are you just humoring me?"

Turning her head, she found Toby staring at her intently. "I mean it, Toby. Things aren't great, but I know this is where I belong. I'm a shifter now, a mated one!"

"So where is he? Cage seems to think Bass is a douche."

Katalina burst out laughing. "He'll be back soon, I think. I can't believe Cage said that."

Toby laughed and gasped, his face scrunching up. "Stop making me laugh!"

"But douche? I can think of many things Cage would call him, but not that."

"Well, he didn't say *douche* exactly, but it's what he meant."

They were both laughing when Bass walked in. "I hope you're not talking about me."

Katalina smiled wickedly. "Depends. Are you a douche?"

"A douche? Is that even a word?" Bass asked.

Katalina nearly choked for laughing.

Toby reached over to grab his phone. "According to Urban Dictionary, *douche* or *douche bag* means: 'Someone who has surpassed the levels of jerk and asshole, however not yet reached fucker or motherfucker.'"

Toby's mother chose that moment to walk in, a plate of food in her hand. "Toby!" she gasped, looking outraged.

Katalina bit her lip to keep from laughing. "Right, I best be off."

"Already?" Toby whined, the look on his face saying *don't leave me alone with my fussing mother.*

"Sorry, Toby, I've lots of important badass things to do." She lifted his legs gently, getting up.

Once out of the room, Bass blocked her path, a questioning look on his face. "Badass?"

"A joke. So you weren't gone very long. Did everything go okay?"

"I left them on the border of Dark Shadow land. Someone will find them soon, but it's not patrolled regularly. I'm not ready to face my father yet."

"Okay," she answered, not sure she'd ever be ready to face his father. "Come on. Let's raid the kitchen. I'm starving."

He stopped her as she was about to push the door open. "Hey, Kat, about before."

Katalina stopped his words with a kiss. "Leave it for tonight. I just want to forget about everything until tomorrow."

# CHAPTER 28

Sitting at the table when Jackson came in, Katalina rubbed her arms as a cold gust blew in. The night had grown dark and there was a chill in the air that even Katalina felt.

"It's pretty nippy out there. I reckon we'll have another dumping of snow before winter's out."

Cage walked into the kitchen. He ignored Katalina and Bass. "All quiet out there?" he asked Jackson.

"Yep, you shouldn't have any problems. Tate's just arrived from out of town. He's a bit inexperienced, but four eyes are better than two."

Cage gave a thoughtful nod as he went out into the cold night.

"What have you got there?" Jackson asked Katalina, looking at her plate.

"Sandwich," she replied slowly, as if he were dumb.

"Looks good." His hand shot out, so quickly it was a blur. Katalina looked down at her plate; the last half of her sandwich was gone.

"Hey!"

"What? I'm hungry. Been out there the last hour making sure you're safe. Least you can do is feed me." He smiled at her. It was the first time she'd seen an emotion on his face other than anger or irritation.

She almost laughed, but stopped the urge before it happened. No way was she just going to start playing happy family with him. He'd have to work harder than a smile and stealing her food.

"Well, enjoy it." Her chair scraped back loudly. "We're going to bed." She gave Bass no other option. Pulling his hand, she dragged him to his feet. He quickly reached out for the last of his food to take with him.

"Bed?" Jackson spluttered.

"Yeah, you know, the place you go to sleep," she said sarcastically.

"With him?" He pointed stupidly at Bass.

"Yes, him! Mated, remember?"

"I'm not sure a father should approve of this."

Katalina was already half out of the kitchen, pushing Bass ahead of her. She looked back at him, a sweet smile coating her lips. "Good thing you don't act like a father then."

She'd gotten halfway up the stairs by the time Jackson thought of a retort. Katalina didn't listen. She wasn't about to make Jackson's life easy. He had a lot to make up for.

"That was a little uncalled for," Bass muttered when Kat pushed him into the room she'd stayed in before and shut the door.

She stood with her back to the door, hands cupped behind her. "Oh, stop. I'm not about to start calling him *Dad* and playing happy family just because he's decided to be a little less of an ass."

"Yes, but Katalina, we need him to accept us. Do you not think treating him with a little respect would go a long way? He's an alpha after all."

"Honestly, I don't care. He could be the freaking president and I'd still treat him the same. Now, stop with all the words. Go away, Sebastian Evernight, and bring me my big bad shadow wolf."

"Big bad shadow wolf?"

"Yes," she smiled, reaching up for a kiss.

Bass pulled back, a little breathless. His eyes filled with the hunger he felt for Katalina. "I'm not sure you'd like him tonight. He's feeling rather territorial surrounded by all these River Runs and that pup who can't keep his eyes off you."

"Pup?"

"Cage."

Katalina laughed. "He's a year younger than you, hardly a pup."

"Hmm . . ." he growled. "I'm not in the mood to be sweet and gentle." He pushed her against the door, kissing his way down her neck. "I could do with a run actually," he murmured against her skin.

"No!" She pulled his mouth toward hers, claiming another kiss. "You are not going anywhere tonight. Make me forget, Bass. For one night, I don't want to think about what you have to do, or how it felt to fight and taste the enemy's blood in my mouth. I just want to forget it all."

Bass reached out, pulling her against him with the speed of his wolf.

Katalina squealed and laughed as she melted against the hard contours of his body.

He kissed her roughly, invading her mouth, filling her mind with only him. Katalina broke away with a gasp, desperate for air.

"You want to forget. I can make you forget." His voice brushed against the sensitive skin on her neck. He kissed and nipped and she could do nothing but surrender to him.

He kissed her softly at first, his hands gentle as they explored the curves of her body. He invaded all her senses: the feel of him, the scent of his skin, the taste of him in her mouth. As his kisses grew more urgent, his hands gripping her tighter, Katalina's brain started to kick back into drive.

*Am I ready for this? Has he done this before? OMG, what am I doing?*

Bass pulled back, sensing her hesitation. Katalina looked into his heated eyes and saw the love, the desire within the dark depths.

"Kat, what's wrong?" he asked softly.

She stared at him, unsure what to say. Despite a million things running through her brain, not a single coherent thought left her mouth.

"I, I . . ."

"Hey"—he brushed a thumb over her cheek—"we don't have to do anything you don't want to."

"No, no, I want to. It's just, I . . . I've never done this before, and well, you know, we need . . ." Katalina felt her cheeks heat with embarrassment. She dropped her eyes to the floor, wishing it would open up and swallow her.

His finger brushed under her chin, lifting her head to meet his gaze. "Neither have I."

"Oh," was all she could manage.

"And I'm guessing you're referring to needing this?" He pulled a condom from his pocket and held it up for her to see.

Katalina nodded yes, her eyes glued to the condom, the blush on her cheeks spreading down to her chest.

"Kat, I'm not pressuring you into anything."

"I know." She reached up and kissed him, gently, then more firmly as she wrapped her hands into the silk of his hair.

He kissed her back and led her toward the bed. Bass lowered her gently, never taking his loving eyes off Katalina as they slowly lost their clothes.

"Wait!" Katalina pulled back. "How long have you had that?"

Bass shook his head and smiled. "I picked it up on the drive back here. You know, just in case."

"So you've been expecting this to happen?"

"We're mated, Kat. It was going to happen eventually, and it's not like I can just run to the store in the middle of a war."

Katalina laughed quietly. "Okay. Kiss me."

"As you wish, my winter wolf," he said with a mischievous smile.

That night, with the winds howling, promising a storm, Katalina stared into the dark eyes of her shadow wolf. His hands explored her slowly, with a gentleness he possessed only for her. His kisses were urgent, wanting, but each one voiced a silent proclamation of his love. And with each kiss, each lingering touch, he mapped out the story of their hearts.

*****

Katalina opened her eyes to dim light filtering through the window. She had a clear view outside as they'd fallen asleep with the curtains open.

She turned slightly, moving her body just a fraction so she wouldn't wake Bass. His limbs were tangled around hers, his arms a protective cage. The warmth from his bare skin seeped into her as if he were the most intimate blanket.

She sighed, closing her eyes briefly as memories of the night before drifted through her mind like the sweetest of dreams. She felt different this morning, as if last night had been the final step in forever sealing Bass to her soul.

She smiled, clinging to the happiness and love swirling through her blood. She never wanted this feeling to end. She wanted to lie with Bass forever, safe in his arms. Sleeping, relaxed and peaceful, he wore no mask. No shifter politics clouded his eyes. At that moment, he was just Bass, her shadow wolf. It was just the two of them: the shadow wolf and the winter wolf.

His eyes opened slowly, his long lashes casting shadows as they lifted. Dark pools stared at her, drank her in.

"Hey." He broke the silence, his voice the softest caress.

"Hi." She couldn't keep the silly smile from her face.

"You look happy."

"I am. The happiest."

"You are so beautiful," he whispered, kissing her shoulder.

She felt heat flood her cheeks.

"And very cute when you blush," he continued.

"Stop it," she laughed.

They paused at the sound of the door opening and closing downstairs. Muffled voices whispered toward them.

"What time is it?" Bass asked her.

"Sixish. Seems earlier because of the snow, I think."

Bass glanced toward the window. "Great," he muttered. The snow fell fast and unrelenting, blocking the sky in a blanket of ever-moving white. "I suppose we should get up," he said.

"No, not yet, please. Let me bask in this moment a little longer."

He smiled wickedly, rolling on top of her. "A little longer," he murmured. He kissed and nipped down her neck, and for a little while, Katalina didn't think of what lay ahead. All thoughts left her, until the feel and touch of Bass consumed her.

# CHAPTER 29

Katalina stood on the porch with Bass and Jackson. The three of them looked at the snow soundlessly falling. Like a million frozen feathers floating to the earth, the snow built layer by layer, and with each layer came more dread.

"Are you sure we can't just go tomorrow?" Katalina asked.

"No, Kat, my father will know about me ordering his men away. The longer he waits for me, the greater his anger will become."

"Don't worry, Kat. I'll protect you," Jackson said to her. He patted her on the shoulder, but Katalina pulled away.

"It's not me I'm worried about." She could barely contain the anger building inside, making her wolf restless.

Bass stood in front of her, momentarily blocking her from the weather. "I promise you, we'll get through this."

"Don't make promises you can't keep, Bass. The best outcome for today is killing your father, and that isn't an outcome I'm very happy about," she answered glumly, wishing there was some way this could end differently.

"He may listen."

"Yes, and you sound so convinced of that," she muttered.

"Maybe she should stay here," Jackson suggested.

"Maybe *you* should stay here," she spat, glaring at him over Bass's shoulder. "Surely, you'll just be considered a threat?"

"Do not forget, daughter of mine, you are River Run, too."

Bass took hold of her hands. She pulled her eyes away from Jackson and tried to rein in her temper. "He needs to come to confirm he is willing to allow peace, and I need to know someone else is there watching your back. We are going to be surrounded by Dark Shadow. If something happens to me, I need to know you will be safe."

"You just promised me everything was going to be all right," she pointed out.

"It is," Bass confirmed. She opened her lips to argue but he closed his mouth over hers, her muffled words getting lost in their mingled breath.

"Stop stalling. Let's go!" Jackson grunted.

"Fine!" she snapped, focusing her anger on Jackson.

Katalina walked to the truck as large flakes swirled around her, landing on her cheeks like frosty kisses. As they drove, she stared out the window, watching the world of white pass her by.

She'd always loved the snow. Quite often, she'd run outside and stand with her arms spread wide, head tilted to the cloud-covered sky with her tongue stuck out to catch the quickly melting flakes. The snow froze time and transformed the world into a fairy-tale landscape, but as she watched the snow today, she couldn't see the fairy tale or the beauty.

"We'll pull over here and walk the rest of the way. With the snow, I don't think the truck's going to get through," Bass said.

Jackson nodded and hopped out. Katalina followed. She held Bass's hand as they walked into the trees. The snow-covered branches above them blocked out the little light there was. For once, she was grateful for her shifter senses and enhanced sight.

They'd been walking for ten long minutes. The snow had stopped falling as they'd walked. Bass and Jackson were vigilant, their eyes scanning one way and another, ears tilted toward the wind to catch distant sounds. Katalina watched them, marveling at how wolflike they seemed, even in human form. She wondered whether she'd ever be that natural, or if she'd always be the outsider who grew up as a human and never quite lost her skin.

She noticed the change in Jackson's body language before she heard the soft tread of footfalls. She tilted her head, trying to hear better, when the air was sucked out of her. Her body moved so fast, her head was spinning when she was set back on her feet.

With a shake of her head, she focused her eyes. Bass moved her behind him, his body angled defensively, one hand pressed against her leg. Jackson was at her back. The energy and the power zapped across the few inches separating them.

Wolves appeared all around them, watching them, but they didn't move to fight.

"I'm here to see my father," Bass said to the wolves, his voice soft, nonthreatening.

"And the River Run alpha?" They all focused on the man who walked into the center of the wolves. He was still in human form, dressed in black, his skin bronzed and his hair long and as black as coal. His brown eyes held a nasty edge, his voice one of malice.

"Malaki," Bass nodded in greeting.

"Thank the heavens. The alpha's prodigal son has returned, and he's brought us a River Run whore and the alpha to play with," he said with a chuckle.

Bass's and Jackson's growls thundered around them, their bodies tensed, ready to attack.

"My father, Malaki," Bass snapped.

"Oh, don't worry. You'll be seeing him. He's looking forward to hearing your explanation for killing your own and ordering his men away. I am too, actually. Care to give me the spoilers?" He laughed again, indicating for them to follow him.

The wolves fanned around them as they walked, never moving more than four feet away at any time. Katalina tried to calm her rapidly beating heart. Bass never took his hand from hers; she was sure he could feel her sweaty palms. She was petrified. Katalina had imagined so many scenarios, but none of them had been as terrifying as this. The farther they walked, the more densely packed the trees became, until their path opened out onto a large open area. The snow had been cleared into piles. Wooden cabins were dotted here and there; men, women, and children stood on their porches, watching them as they walked. Katalina felt like she'd been transported to a horror movie set in a time where men were the leaders and ruled by keeping others under their barbaric thumbs. As she looked around, she realized what Bass had meant. This place, this pack, was nothing like River Run. River Run's compound looked like the most normal place on earth compared to this.

Malaki indicated for them to stop in the center of a circle of cabins. The largest stood in front of them. A huge bonfire to the left cast an orange hue over the ground.

"Son! What have you brought me?" The man who walked out of the largest cabin was a huge, solid brick of a man. Although very wide and with arms like tree trunks, he was clearly a little on the chubby side, his middle as wide as his shoulders. But none of this made him any less intimidating. The power rolling off him prickled against Katalina's skin. Her wolf stirred and rose, her every instinct saying *run!*

Bass didn't say a word as his father walked around them. He appeared calm, his posture lazy even.

"Jackson, how lovely of you to visit, and this must be your daughter. She's the image of her mother, such beauty. What a shame for it to leave this world."

Katalina was struggling for air. Her head felt dizzy, the buzzing in her ears preventing her from concentrating on the predator in front of her.

"She looks terrified, Jackson. Haven't you taught her anything?" Bass's father continued.

Just as she was on the verge of passing out, Bass's soothing presence wrapped around her. He eased the fear inside of her, enabling her to gasp in the needed oxygen.

"Well, everyone has gathered around, Sebastian. Why don't you tell me why the girl clings to your hand like a frightened child?"

"Father, I'd like you to meet Katalina, my mate." Bass stepped to the side slightly, so his father could get a better view.

"Mate?"

"Yes," Bass answered.

Katalina jumped as Bass's father let out a boom of a laugh. No one else seemed to find it funny; the fear and confusion from all those around crept across her skin.

"Did you really think I'd welcome her with open arms, Sebastian? And Jackson, did you think I'd make peace, call an end to the war I've nearly won?"

"Alistair, our children have mated. Maybe it's time we put the past behind us," Jackson said, his voice even.

Bass's father laughed again, his voice bouncing through the silence.

"Did I not teach you better, Sebastian?"

"You taught me many things, Father. How to fight, how to instill fear into others, but most of all, you showed me how I never want to be like you. I will never be a cruel leader who destroys all who question me. I will allow our children to be children. Dark Shadow will no longer be the prison you have created. It will be a home for the Dark Shadow wolves who want to be here."

The atmosphere changed in an instant. Unease, hunger, and death whispered through the air like a mantra.

"Do you challenge me, boy?" his father asked. His face contorted with the venom in his voice; hatred and violence danced in his eyes.

"Alistair Evernight, I challenge you," Bass replied. His voice reflected strength, courage, and promise.

"Which form do you choose?" Alistair asked.

"Man."

Katalina found herself ripped from Bass's hand in an instant. Jackson's arms enclosed her, dragging her from Bass as his father circled around him.

The people around them erupted into excited shouts, their voices barbaric, hungry to see blood spilled.

Alistair lunged toward Bass, his fists clenched, his eyes livid. Katalina watched as Bass danced out of his way, his feet nimble and light as they skated over the ground. The noise around Katalina blurred into the background as she watched them preparing to fight. Her heart boomed in her ears, fear pulsing through her veins.

Trembling, she couldn't look away. Instead she felt herself slowly breaking apart. Jackson still held her, and for once she didn't fight him; he was the only thing keeping her upright.

"Come on, boy. Make a move!" Alistair shouted at his son.

But Bass ignored his father, jumping once more from his reach.

"Why doesn't he fight?" Katalina whispered.

"His father's stronger but he's also older. He'll tire before Bass," Jackson whispered into her ear.

Bass stumbled, leaving himself unprotected. Alistair's fist connected with his jaw. Katalina watched in horror as the impact forced Bass's head backward, his feet nearly going out from under him.

"Oh God, I can't watch this." Katalina turned her head away.

Bass dodged his father's next move by fractions of an inch. Regaining his balance, he jumped away, circling his father again.

Katalina could see the impatience in Alistair's eyes, in the way he moved. It infuriated him that Bass wouldn't fight; it also made him sloppy. He rushed forward, swinging for Bass with a grunt. Again, Bass stepped out of the way. However, this time, when his feet carried on with their dance, his elbow smashed into the back of his father's neck. His father stumbled forward with an angry growl. Spinning around, he charged again.

The dance carried on, Bass moving, never really attacking, and the longer it went on, the angrier Alistair became.

Nico appeared in front of her. "You need to move—now!"

"What? N-Nico?" Katalina stuttered.

Nico never answered her. Jackson shoved her behind himself. The air rushed out of her lungs as chaos erupted.

Nico took her hand. "Come with me!" he shouted, dragging her through the crowd.

"Jackson!" Katalina gasped as Malaki appeared out of nowhere and jumped him.

Katalina felt like a rag doll as Nico dragged and shoved her forward. All around her there was noise: Jackson's growls and grunts; the excited cries of those reveling in this madness; and the screams and cries of children as their mothers carried them away in terror.

Nico's hand felt like a vice as he dragged her through the crowd. She lost sight of Bass for a second and in that time, she felt his terror fill her. His voice called out to her over the crowd, "Katalina!"

She spotted him again through the dozen people blocking her way. Their eyes connected just as a twisted smile appeared across his father's lips. Bass fell to the ground, his head snapping back as he hit the unforgiving earth. Blood splattered from his lips, the fight leaving his eyes.

Katalina watched, fighting against Nico as he tried to get her to safety. His father's foot connected with Bass's gut, sending him flying through the air. He landed like a dead weight, his arms spread awkwardly in front of him.

"Bass!" she gasped, pulling her hand free.

She tried to run, but Jackson appeared in front of her and lifted her off her feet, tucking her under his armpit.

"Bass!" she screamed.

Alistair looked up and smiled at her before looking down at his son in triumph.

Katalina felt her wolf rise to the surface. She struggled from Jackson's hold and found herself pushing through the crowd to get to Bass. She felt the moment he gave up. She felt his defeat, and as her eyes connected with his, she saw the message written in them: *I'm sorry.*

Pure fury surged through her. She pushed aside the people in her way, felt the growl within her building. Katalina broke through to the edge of the circle, directing her angry gaze at Bass. He'd promised her they'd make it through this. He'd said they'd build a new world together, yet he was giving up.

"You promised!" she screamed, her wolf's growl in her tone. "You promised me!" He felt her words like a razor's edge. She took a step toward him. "GET UP!"

Bass moved just a split second before his father would have delivered the deathblow. He jumped to his feet, his body spinning out of the way, and his elbow slammed into Alistair's side. The momentum carried Alistair, already bent forward, to the ground, his face smashing into the slush and mud.

Bass didn't hesitate. He hit his father repeatedly until Alistair was a bloodied mess at Bass's feet. He stood over him, panting from exhaustion.

"It's over, Father. Enough blood has been spilled. Let this be over," Bass said wearily, looking down at his father with pity.

Bass stepped away from Alistair, his eyes seeking Katalina. As he found her, his knees went out from under him. Katalina caught him before he fell.

"I've got you," she whispered, wrapping her arm under his shoulder.

There were hushed whispers all around them. People stared in confusion, looking from Bass to his father.

Katalina heard an audible gasp. She looked up as Bass's father lurched forward, a lethal-looking knife held high in his hand.

They weren't able to move out of the way in time. Bass, injured as he was, couldn't move quickly enough. Katalina screamed as the knife came toward them, glinting in the dim light. Then there was nothing but fur—light-gray fur, sprinkled with white.

The knife hit Jackson as his jaws wrapped around Alistair's throat. They fell together to the ground, neither moving.

"Jackson!" Katalina pulled him off Alistair. "Jackson!" She yanked the knife from his fur. Seconds later, he turned back into his human form.

She could hear Bass talking behind her, but she couldn't concentrate on the words. All she could think was how she couldn't live through losing another parent. It didn't matter how mad she was at him. He couldn't die; he wasn't allowed to leave her again.

"Jackson!"

His eyes opened. "I'll be o . . . kay," he gasped. She pulled her hand away from his body; it was coated in blood.

"Oh God," she whispered.

Jackson coughed, his body convulsing as blood spilled from his mouth.

"Jackson!" Katalina sobbed.

Someone lifted her to her feet as people surrounded him.

"Get off!" she screamed.

"Kat! Kat, look at me!" She focused her eyes on Bass's face. "Let them look after him," he said softly.

Bass swayed on his feet. Nico was there a second later, holding him up. "Wow, pal, I think you need to be in a bed right beside Jackson."

"I can't. I need to contain the fallout."

There was a yell and a child's scream. Fur erupted from skin as the Dark Shadow wolves began to fight one another.

"Enough!" Bass boomed. Immediately, the fighting around them stopped. "I understand some of you are confused, and I understand a lot of you were loyal to my father. I'm nothing like my father and anyone unhappy with me as their alpha is free to leave. I won't stop you and no one will harm you by my orders, but if you do go, remember this: the moment you leave pack land, you are never to come back without prior permission from me. Think carefully about what you want. You have twenty-four hours to decide."

Katalina looked at Bass with pride, pleased he was trying to end this with no more bloodshed.

"I've made my decision," Malaki stepped forward. "I will never follow you, and I'll be damned if you think I'll let you run this pack!" He pushed his way through the crowd, sending people sprawling to the ground.

"No one can challenge the alpha until five days have passed!" an older man said, stepping forward.

"I don't give a shit about rules, old man!" Malaki spat.

"Kat, go!" Bass hissed, pushing her away. Nico vanished into the crowd.

"No, he'll kill you."

"Oh, don't worry, little girl. I'm going to kill you first and make him watch."

His legs tensed to spring. Standing her ground, her arms remained wrapped around Bass. If she was dying, she'd die beside Bass.

Only Malaki never made the leap. The tip of a sword protruded from his chest. A gargled gasp escaped his mouth as the sword was pulled back out, and he dropped to the ground, dead.

"Anyone else have something to say?" Nico asked, wiping the blade of his sword over his leg.

"I do," the older man said, stepping into the center of the circle. "I've been an enforcer for this pack a long time, long enough to remember what it used to be like before Alistair went mad with grief. He destroyed the very fabric of what it means to be a shifter in his bitter quest for vengeance. A pack is meant to be a family, a safe place where you trust your alpha to do what's best for you. It shouldn't be a dictatorship. You shouldn't quiver at the mere sight of your alpha. I know Sebastian is young, but I've known him his whole life, and I stand by him."

He turned and stood in front of Bass. Lowering his head, he said, "I accept you as my alpha." Then his eyes focused on Katalina before dropping again. "I accept you as my alpha's mate."

Bass reached out and squeezed the man's shoulder. "Thank you, Bill."

"Right then, scatter, all of you. Our new alpha needs a doctor," Nico yelled. The crowd froze, silent as they wondered whether to follow Nico's order. "Didn't you hear me? Scatter!" They dispersed like little ants, scurrying here and there until only four men remained, Dark Shadow enforcers.

"Go get fixed up. The politics can wait. We'll patrol and make sure no one starts any trouble," one of the enforcers said.

Bass replied, "I need one of you to go to River Run and let them know what has happened. If any of them would like to come see their alpha, they are to be allowed on our lands and treated with the same respect as our own. Understood?"

"Yes," the enforcers murmured in unison.

"Come on," Katalina said. He'd been leaning more heavily against her with every passing minute. "Little help, Nico."

*****

Katalina sat alone on the deck of the doctor's cabin. The snow had stopped falling a while ago and the sun had come out in the wake of the clouds. Bass and Jackson were both asleep after receiving a sedative so that they would rest and heal. William and Graham had come back with the Dark Shadow enforcers. They'd treated the Dark Shadows with respect, but Katalina could see the doubt in their eyes. They refused to leave their alpha's side, Graham standing at the foot of Jackson's bed as a guard, with William on a chair, his braced leg propped up.

Exhausted, Katalina didn't have the brainpower to think about all that had happened.

"You might as well come sit with me instead of lurking behind corners, Nico."

Nico flopped down beside her. "There go my killer spy skills."

Katalina smiled. "Do you ever get tired?" she asked.

"Not really. How'd you spot me?" he asked.

She frowned. "Not sure—just sensed you there, I guess."

"Didn't think you'd have wolf senses yet, with only just changing."

"Bass tell you everything?"

"Not always, but he seemed to think you needed to be looked after."

"I'm getting stronger every day. Though I haven't the energy to get up, let alone defend myself."

"Well, that's why you have me! Bodyguard extraordinaire."

Katalina covered her mouth as she yawned.

"Why don't you go to sleep?" Nico asked.

"I don't have a bed."

"Go and curl up with Bass. No one will stop you."

"All right." Katalina dragged her sore, tired body up. She paused before walking into the cabin. "Hey, Nico, you'll stick around, right?"

"Bodyguard extraordinaire, remember?" Nico laughed.

Katalina lay gently on the bed, as close to Bass as she could get without touching him. As she closed her eyes, she smiled, thinking that maybe, just maybe, they could carve out a world they both belonged to.

# EPILOGUE

## ONE MONTH LATER

Katalina couldn't quite believe they'd pulled it off. There were people here actually enjoying themselves. She wandered through the party filled with pack members from both Dark Shadow and River Run. Listening to their conversations and their laughter provided a sense of contentment she'd yet to experience since her parents' deaths. Music pulsed through the air, the timbre resonating through her blood. The huge fire crackled and spit, casting its warmth and glow over them all, and the smell of food wafting through the air, mixing with the scents all around her, made her sigh with satisfaction. Over the past month, she'd grown into her wolf. Sometimes it amazed her, seeing how different the world was through the eyes of her wolf; the wolf used more than just sight. Scent, sound, touch: all of these things guided her through the woods, through her new life.

Someone called her name. Katalina paused, looking for the face to match the voice. Her hand raised, a smile spreading across her lips. "Hey," she called back, carrying on with her wandering. Being an alpha's mate wasn't the easiest responsibility. She sometimes felt as if she'd aged ten years overnight. Pack members from both Dark Shadow and River Run came to her for advice. They asked her opinion on the situations of everyday pack life. This new life was so vastly different from her old one, but in many ways it felt completely right. She might not know anything about the way a pack should be run, but she had her real world opinions, and so far they'd gotten her through some pretty difficult situations.

"Kat! Kat!" A second later, Toby's arms wrapped around her shoulders. "Come with me to get some food! I'm starving. Just came off my patrol."

Katalina changed her direction, smiling at Toby's infectious enthusiasm. "So how was it? All quiet?"

"Yeah, some of the old fogies from Dark Shadow are hanging around the borders. The idiots are missing out on this awesome party! Seriously, Kat, this was the best idea."

"Thanks, Toby. I'm pretty pleased with the outcome. Is Cage coming?" she asked hopefully.

Smile dropping for a second, Toby answered sadly, "No, he's doing double shifts. I don't think he'll come after."

"Do you think he'll ever forgive me?" she asked, feeling responsible for hurting Cage.

"I'm sure he will, Kat. Let's not talk about him now. We're at a party," Toby replied, brightening.

"Katalina." She'd hear that voice anywhere, through the loudest of parties, the biggest of crowds. Her smile changed as she sought him out, her shadow wolf. He still took her breath away. Her heart raced when he returned her smile, contentment filling her soul.

"Go on then!" Toby grumbled. "I'll grab food and come find you."

"Okay." She planted a kiss on his cheek before hurrying off. "Hey, you," she murmured, wrapping her arms around Bass's neck. "Finished all your important alpha duties?"

"Just one more left," he said, before claiming her lips with his.

"Oh, what's that?" she asked, hoping he didn't have to leave again.

"To keep all the wandering eyes off my beautiful mate."

Katalina laughed as she dropped her hands away. "Come on. Nico has claimed the best seating." She took his hand and pulled him toward the far edge of the party.

Nico sat lounging on a sofa, his eyes fixed on a girl who stood by the fire.

"Who's that?" Katalina whispered as they approached.

"Oh, that's Olivia. Nico's had a crush on her forever."

"She doesn't feel the same?"

"She's pureblood. Nico's half."

"So? That's not an explanation!" Katalina snapped.

"No, not any more, my feisty girl," Bass chuckled.

Katalina jabbed her finger in his side and ran off laughing. She jumped onto the sofa next to Nico. "Hey!"

"Hey, yourself," Nico answered.

"So, bodyguard extraordinaire, why don't you stop staring and go talk to her?" Katalina teased.

"Talk to who?" Nico asked.

"Olivia," Bass answered for him.

"Stop telling your mate all my secrets!" Nico grumbled. "And I'll talk to her when I'm good and ready. No interfering, you two."

Katalina laughed, ruffling Nico's perfectly styled hair, much to his disgust. "I have magic powers, Nico. He can't help but tell me."

"You two are disgusting, you know that."

"You'll be disgusting too, when you've finally worked up the nerve to speak to *her*!" Katalina countered.

"I said, stay out of it, all right?"

They didn't answer. Instead, Katalina crawled onto Bass's lap, kissing him. "I missed you," she whispered.

"I was only gone an hour," he whispered back.

"I still missed you."

Bass grazed his mouth over her ear. "I missed you, too."

"Will you two get off each other?" Jackson growled.

Katalina moved her legs and curled up against Bass's side, resting her head on his shoulder. She looked up at Jackson. "Will you stop being a grumpy ass?"

"Who's a grumpy ass?" Toby asked as he took a seat next to Nico, his plate piled with enough food for two.

"Jackson," Katalina confirmed.

Toby burst out laughing, spitting food everywhere.

"The youth of today," Bill muttered as he approached them, shaking his head.

"Yes, they have no respect," Jackson agreed, shaking Bill's hand.

"Everything all right?" Bass asked Bill, his second-in-command.

"Yes, all running smoothly so far."

Katalina slapped Bass across the chest. "No work talk. You've clocked out."

"An alpha never clocks out," Jackson stated.

"In your world maybe," Katalina countered, glaring at him, daring him to respond.

"And which world do you live in, daughter of mine?"

"The real world," she said with a smile.

"The real world?" he repeated.

"Yep, you should come try it out sometime," Nico added.

Jackson shook his head, looking at Bill. "You have any idea what they are talking about?"

"Not a clue. Bass?"

"Oh, it's a real thing and once you've been there, you'll never want to go back," Bass told them. Then, for Katalina's ears only, he added, "You'll find the most exquisite things in the real world, and once you've found them, you'll never let them go."

He kissed her with a lazy hunger, dragging her back onto his lap. The others around them whistled and grumbled, but Katalina and Bass didn't care.

Pulling away from their searing kiss, Katalina linked her hands around his neck and surveyed those around her. Nico was stealing food from Toby while Jackson and Bill stood with their arms crossed, looking serious, but she was convinced they were secretly having fun. Things weren't simple here, and she still felt the sharp pain of losing her parents, but this was home and she was happy. "We did it, you know," she murmured against his neck.

"Did what?" he asked her.

"Carved out our own little piece of the world."

Bass looked at the smiling faces around him, the most unlikely of friends.

"Yeah, we did, didn't we?"

# ACKNOWLEDGMENTS

I'd like to start off by thanking you, the reader. Without you I wouldn't be here, publishing my third book, with another two in the pipeline for release next year. I never imagined I'd reach this far, and every time I read your messages and reviews, it still feels surreal.

I'd like to thank the awesome ladies on my street team. You know who you are and I love you! Thank you for loving and sharing my work with such passion.

Thank you to my wonderful family, for your continued support and encouragement, and a special thanks to Caelan, who was four weeks old when I started writing this. Thank you for being such a good baby; I'd never have completed the first draft in two months if you hadn't slept so well.

And lastly, to the bloggers of the world: you rock!

# ABOUT THE AUTHOR

*Photo © 2012 Lauren Joy Photography*

Rachel M. Raithby started her writing career in 2013 and hasn't looked back. She draws her inspiration from the many places she has lived and traveled, as well as from her love of the paranormal and thriller movies. She can often be found hiding out with a good book or writing more fast-paced and thrilling stories where love always conquers all. A Brit who left the UK in 2008, she resides in a quiet town in Queensland, Australia, with her family.

Made in the USA
Middletown, DE
22 November 2015